BEYOND WALLS

BEYOND WALLS

Theatre Passe Muraille 1968–1975

PETER JOBIN

with period photographs by
Lionel Douglas & Robert Nasmith

and a foreword
by David Ferry

The Porcupine's Quill

Library and Archives Canada Cataloguing in Publication

Jobin, Peter, 1944–2018, author

Beyond Walls : Theatre Passe Muraille, 1968–1975 / Peter Jobin ; with period photographs by Lionel Douglas & Robert Naismith and a foreword by David Ferry.

ISBN 978-0-88984-418-6 (softcover)

1. Theatre Passe Muraille — History. 2. Theatrical companies — Ontario — Toronto — History. I. Title.

PN2306.T62T45 2018 792.09713'541 C2018-904254-0

1 2 3 • 20 19 18

Published by The Porcupine's Quill, 68 Main Street, PO Box 160, Erin, Ontario N0B 1T0. http://porcupinesquill.ca

Page 2: poster, *The Farm Show* with Anne Anglin, Paul Thompson, Miles Potter and Fina MacDonell, 1972–73.

Copyedited by Chandra Wohleber. Represented in Canada by Canadian Manda. Trade orders are available from University of Toronto Press.

We acknowledge the support of the Ontario Arts Council and the Canada Council for the Arts for our publishing program. The financial support of the Government of Canada is also gratefully acknowledged.

Canada Council for the Arts Conseil des arts du Canada

Canada

ONTARIO ARTS COUNCIL
CONSEIL DES ARTS DE L'ONTARIO
an Ontario government agency
un organisme du gouvernement de l'Ontario

Ontario
Ontario Media Development Corporation

CONTENTS

THEATRE PASSE MURAILLE

Beyond Walls is dedicated to Des McAnuff,
youngest and brightest of the artists who led the Toronto scene.

Des inspired me to write this history
and generously supported my efforts.

I really enjoyed it all.

— *Peter Jobin*, June 2018

ACRONYMS

CODCO: comedy troupe from Newfoundland founded in 1973, originally as a theatrical revue.

DDF: the Dominion Drama Festival promoted amateur theatre in Canada from 1932 to 1978.

FREE: Toronto Free Theatre was founded in 1971 by John Palmer, Martin Kinch and Tom Hendry; subsequently merged with Centre Stage in 1987 by TFT's artistic director Guy Sprung and Centre Stage's artistic director Bill Glassco to form the Canadian Stage Company.

FUT: Festival of Underground Theatre proposed by Henry Tarvainen; August 19 to September 6, 1970, at the St Lawrence Centre on Front Street.

GNTM: Great North Theatre Management, started by Ralph Zimmerman.

LAMDA: London (England) Academy of Music and Dramatic Art.

LIP: Local Initiatives Program, introduced by finance minister Edgar Benson in 1972 to create jobs for unemployed workers in the winter months.

NDG: New Directors' Group, founded at Rochdale College in 1970 by Jim Garrard and Martin Kinch who were later joined by Ken Gass and John Palmer, then by Martin Brenzell and Henry Tarvainen.

NDWT: acronym for a theatre company founded by Keith Turnbull that toured *The Donnellys* across Canada in 1975. The initials stand for Ne'er Do Well Thespians.

OFY: Opportunities for Youth, a program introduced by Prime Minister Pierre Trudeau in 1971 to address the issue of student unemployment.

TNP: Roger Planchon's Théâtre National Populaire—a 'people's theatre' that aimed to bring culture to working-class audiences beyond the Parisian boulevards.

TPM: Theatre Passe Muraille.

TWP: Toronto Workshop Productions; one of the first important Alternative and Experimental Theatre troupes, founded by George Luscombe in Toronto in 1959.

FOREWORD

A theatre free of distinctions between actor and spectator, between 'inside' and 'outside' the theatre, between drama as one art form, music as another and dancing as yet another.

—Jim Garrard, describing his proposed company in a report outlining his plans for a drama program at Rochdale College

One of my favourite stories from Theatre Passe Muraille lore revolves around a 1969 adaptation by John Palmer of *Richard III*, with a cast of twelve, directed by Martin Kinch, that was rehearsed but never performed at TPM due to a funding crisis. As Peter Jobin relates in *Beyond Walls*, one of the actors in the *Richard* cast, Bernice Gai Hune (*Tom Paine*) clung to the back of Don Steinhouse (*A Bond Honoured*; *Ubu Raw*) in order to portray Richard's hump.[1] That kind of upending-the-traditional-approach to theatre in general and to Shakespeare in particular (as staged at Stratford) was near to the beating heart of my generation of Canadian actors, writers and directors intent on 'reinventing' the theatre.

As a young actor coming to Toronto after graduating from the

1 I am indebted to Bernice Gai Hune's son Nicholas Hune-Brown for the narrative of his mother's portrayal in a 2005 paper for ENGL 431: Canadian Shakespeare (for Professor Leanore Lieblein, McGill University).

National Theatre School of Canada in 1973 I was introduced to a very exciting theatre scene. I had just finished workshopping a new play about the Donnellys of Lucan, Ontario, fame by James Reaney with Keith Turnbull and a group of actors (about to become the nucleus of the NDWT Co.) in Halifax. I had been offered a role in the Toronto premiere production of *Sticks and Stones, The Donnellys Part One* at Tarragon Theatre as well as the title role in David Freeman's *You're Gonna Be Alright Jamie Boy* to be directed by Bill Glassco. What's more, I had turned down good roles at the Stratford Festival, including a lead role in a production slated to tour Australia starring Bill Hutt, in order to work at the fledgling Tarragon. What was wrong with me? What a bad career move, many a person informed me.

The early '70s were heady times in Canadian theatre and the idea of doing new Canadian plays at an 'alternative' theatre for $50 a week was far more exciting than 'getting swallowed' by the Stratford machine doing plays by dead foreign playwrights. And the work in Toronto *was* exciting. A group of small theatres was telling stories on their stages that a nationalistic generation (many of us fuelled by recent experiences creating Opportunities for Youth (OFY) or Local Initiative Projects (LIP) funded[2] work) could relate

---

2 'In the spring of 1971 the Prime Minister [Pierre Trudeau] launched the Opportunities for Youth program as part of a series of programs to address the problem of student unemployment. The following fall the Finance Minister [Edgar Benson] introduced the Local Initiatives Program as part of a larger Special Employment Plan designed to create jobs for unemployed workers in the winter months.' From 'Making Work: Federal Job Creation Policy in the 1970s', Jennifer Marguerite Keck. (A Doctor of Philosophy thesis submitted to the Graduate Department of Social Work, University of Toronto. Retrieved from https://www.collectionscanada.gc.ca/obj/s4/f2/dsk3/ftp04/NQ27793.pdf 06/03/2018.)

to. There was an almost evangelistic fervour about some of us. Many of the productions were of new Canadian plays, either by playwrights in residence or collectively created at Tarragon, Factory Theatre Lab, Theatre Second Floor, Toronto Workshop Productions, Free Theatre, Theatre Passe Muraille or Global Village. And the audiences for those stories were also young and desirous of edgy, experimental, Canadian-created theatre. The effect of the huge increase in new Canadian stories in particular was felt by even the 'established' theatres such as Toronto Arts Productions (now Canadian Stage) and Stratford, which both started to program new Canadian scripts into their seasons as well.

And there was a real kind of competition among the theatres that were telling these stories. I remember playing in a football game down in Cabbagetown near the Riverdale Farm between the Tarragon *Sticks and Stones, The Donnellys Part One* cast and the Passe Muraille *Them Donnellys* cast (which had as an actor/player ex–Edmonton Eskimos running back Bob O'Ree ... nephew of the NHL's first African Canadian player, Willie O'Ree). We played for two hours straight to a 0-0 tie. *THAT* was competition! However we all retired from the pitch to break bread and imbibe together at a house on Winchester Street where about six of us in the Tarragon *Donnellys* were living collectively. The competition between companies was based, I think, on the various theatrical philosophies of the directors: written and literary new Canadian work (Tarragon/Factory) versus collective and populist work (TPM/TWP) versus experimental international and local work (FREE Theatre, where tickets were, briefly, literally free).

To a Newfoundlander like myself it was intriguing that Keith Turnbull (NDWT Co/Tarragon), Paul Thompson (TPM) and Martin Kinch (FREE Theatre) had all started out in London, Ontario, together (Turnbull had started, and ran, Summer Theatre 65, the first summer theatre dedicated to all Canadian plays) and all had worked under John Hirsch at Stratford. There was a definite competitive edge among them all.[3]

As an actor, of course, I was willing (and interested) in working at all these theatres. I can never forget approaching Paul Thompson and asking if he would consider me for a role at TPM and he told me that he couldn't because he believed, artistically and politically, that as a Newfoundlander I should go home and help build theatre there with people like the CODCO or MUMMERS artists. The idea that I might be pursuing a course that was aesthetically essential to me seemed beyond him at the time.[4]

There were a lot of young and exciting actors building the second wave of post–WW II actors in Toronto at the time (if I can refer to the Don Harron, William Hutt, Millie Hall, Douglas Campbell generation as the first wave). This was a generation slated to become true lifetime professional theatre artists. To support our generation there was this growing alternative theatre scene as well as a growing film and TV industry and associated developments such as big actor management companies. (Great North Theatre Management, started by Ralph Zimmerman is one that comes to mind … Ralph had been involved with FREE Theatre and GNTM represented many of the actors who had worked there, such as Saul Rubinek, Nick Mancuso, Kim Cattrall.)

---

3 Though Turnbull once told me that Paul Thompson had literally saved his life when he'd turned up extremely broke and ill in Lyon, France. Thompson took him in and nursed him while assisting Hirsch at Roger Planchon's Théâtre National Populaire (TNP — a 'people's theatre' that aimed to bring culture to working-class audiences beyond the Parisian boulevards). It was based in the Lyon suburb of Villeurbanne.

4 Of course I later realized that he may simply have not found me to be a very interesting actor and was letting me off the hook.

One of the exciting actors who worked out of FREE Theatre as a founding artist was Peter Jobin. Another who worked at FREE early on was Des McAnuff.

So it was such a pleasant surprise when, in 2016, I bumped into Peter and discovered that he had done some work, with financial support from Des, on a book about the alternative theatre scene in Toronto, 1968–1975. Its working title was 'Radical Stages'.

I was sharing a story with Peter at the time about having recently been to the Cameron House to visit a mutual friend, Robert Nasmith, to look at his incredible collection of photographs of Rochdale College and of Passe Muraille productions. Robert had been a combat photographer in Vietnam and so had an excellent photographic eye, but he had also been a friend of another fine photographer, Lionel Douglas, who had shot many production stills at TPM over the years. Lionel had passed in 1979, but Nasmith is the executor of his estate and so has created quite an archive of his work.

Peter immediately mentioned the 'Radical Stages' project and that he had only finished one section ... a section dealing with Theatre Passe Muraille. Knowing that the 50th anniversary of TPM was coming up, I suggested to Peter (and soon to Robert) that we put photos and text together in a kind of chapbook. They both liked the idea. I later reached out to Tim Inkster at the Porcupine's Quill for advice on how to do a chapbook. Without blinking, he suggested he might be able to do it.

So here we are.

Except, I regret to say, here we are, without Peter. He was so chuffed that this book was being published. When I mentioned that Tim Inkster had decided to publish *Beyond Walls*, he said with a droll tone so well known by his friends, 'F____k, who knew it was so easy to get published.' He was looking forward to the book launch. It was in his calendar as a night to pop champagne corks.

Peter died in his sleep in August 2018. So he won't make the book launch. He sends his regrets. Thankfully we have his account of TPM that follows.

I love the easy and flowing prose in Peter's story. He moved from acting to screen writing in the '70s and his career writing for the screen has clearly taught him the art of the self-edit, with short and clear sentences that move the story along. Thanks to him, and thanks to Robert Nasmith for his generous help with the photos. Thanks of course to the late Lionel Douglas for his body of work shooting the theatre of Toronto. Thanks too to the multitude of artists who have built, maintained and evolved Theatre Passe Muraille. It is a national treasure.

David Ferry, Toronto 2018

Paul Thompson's 40th birthday with (left to right) Linda Griffiths, Paul, Severn Thompson. 1980. Photo with permission, Helena Wilson.

BEYOND WALLS

Theatre Passe Muraille 1968–1975

Paul Thompson, moving in a blur,

as the Clinton audience at *The Farm Show* awaits the spectacle, 1972.

Photo courtesy of R. Nasmith Archives.

INTRODUCTION

Toronto Theatre in 1968

In the 1950s, new models for Canadian theatre were developed, combining local community business and cultural objectives. Ontario's Stratford Festival was founded in 1953, Winnipeg's Manitoba Theatre Centre in 1958. The critical and financial success of these two theatres encouraged a regional theatre movement across North America. Over the next ten years, major theatres were established in Canadian cities from Halifax to Vancouver. Financial support was supplied by the Federal Government's Canada Council, founded in 1957.

In Toronto, English Canada's largest city, British and American touring theatre companies still played to enthusiastic audiences; at the Mirvish family's Royal Alexandra Theatre, and the new O'Keefe Centre, opened in 1960. Amateur theatre thrived at the University of Toronto's Hart House Theatre and the University Alumnae Theatre. In nearby cottage country, summer stock companies such as the Red Barn Theatre and the Straw Hat Players flourished.

Founded by the Davis theatre family (Murray, Barbara [later Chilcott] and Donald) in 1953, the Crest Theatre produced regularly over a period of ten years. The plays were mostly British, although a few new Canadian works by Robertson Davies and Mavor Moore also appeared. The Canadian Players was started in 1953 by Stratford Festival co-founder Tom Patterson, and Festival actor Douglas Campbell. They intended to create a classical touring company that would offer winter employment to members of the Festival. By the 1957 season, the Canadian Players had solid bookings across Canada and the United States, spreading the reputation of the Stratford Festival and Canadian classical theatre through North America.

But, by 1965, Toronto *Globe and Mail* critic Herbert Whittaker wrote of the Canadian Players, 'The acting itself deteriorated and the purpose of the company seemed to get lost in the struggle to survive.' Critical coverage of the Crest Theatre also became more negative, led by the *Toronto Star*'s Nathan Cohen. In 1964, the Canada Council rejected the Crest's funding application, citing weak management and artistic direction. Within two years, the Crest Company was closed.

In the fall of 1965, Marigold Charlesworth and Jean Roberts produced a final Canadian Players season at the Central Library Theatre. O'Casey's *The Playboy of the Western World*, starring Martha Henry and Douglas Rain; and Max Frisch's *The Fire Raisers* (or *The Firebugs*), starring Rain and Powys Thomas, received raves. But by January 1966, the limited capacity of the theatre led to an early closure of the season. The only local professional theatre in Toronto was now Toronto Workshop Productions, founded in 1959 by George Luscombe.

In 1950, Luscombe had travelled to England, searching for professional theatre experience. Near the end of 1952, he was hired by Joan Littlewood, director and producer of the Theatre Workshop Company at the Theatre Royal in Stratford East, London. At the age of twenty-six, he made the connection that would change his life. After three years at the Theatre Royal, he returned to Toronto, bringing with him Joan Littlewood's techniques of stylized movement and script development through company improvisation.

In December 1959, Workshop Productions opened two one-act plays directed by George Luscombe, in the basement studio of a printer's shop at 47 Fraser Avenue, in Toronto's west end. A second double bill opened in May 1960, including the Toronto play *Burlap Bags*, which received favourable reviews. Over the next eight years,

Luscombe developed a dozen new plays with his acting company, some more successful than others. In February 1961, *Hey, Rube!* opened to excellent reviews and enthusiastic word-of-mouth. The tiny basement theatre was filled to capacity. *Toronto Star* critic Nathan Cohen wrote that *Hey, Rube!* was 'an exhilarating adventure among the theatre arts' which 'stands head and shoulders above most drama productions shown in Toronto.' The Workshop had achieved its first undeniable success and was now a destination for Toronto audiences.

Globe and Mail critic Herbert Whittaker wrote that Luscombe was 'the most dedicated and original creative talent working in our theatre.' His declared interest in new Canadian plays attracted younger writers. Montreal writer Jack Winter worked as the Workshop's dramaturge and playwright for more than ten years, adapting plays by Aristophanes, Pirandello and Büchner, as well as his own original works. Renamed Toronto Workshop Productions in 1964, Luscombe's company stayed in its basement for the next five years, producing two plays each season.

All Luscombe productions were rewritten and remounted many times. In 1961, Toronto Workshop made a six-month tour of Ontario. The TWP was awarded its first Canada Council operating grant in 1963, and reorganized as a professional Actors' Equity company. From 1964 to 1967, the company made summer visits to the Stratford Festival, playing in a tent near the Festival Theatre. TWP toured to Ontario universities, including York, Queen's and Waterloo, and was the only Toronto theatre company invited to appear at Montreal's Expo 67.

In 1967, a central downtown location was rented at 12 Alexander Street. The company built a new 300-seat arena space within a month, and began previews on December 31, with *Gentlemen Be Seated*, a minstrel-style show focusing on America's black versus white racial conflict. TWP was the first Toronto theatre to use its acting company to develop new Canadian plays and their reputation was growing. Both Luscombe and TWP were now unique Toronto institutions. For the company's regular playwright, Jack Winter, 'there is no one in the business now worth working for except George.'

The Canada Council and the Province of Ontario Council of the Arts were about to publish a joint report, 'The Awkward Stage', concluding that Toronto was, in its own citizens' minds, an undeveloped theatrical community. The coming development of Toronto theatre would be a new, quite distinctive movement, with different leaders, different theatres and very different visions. A new generation of Canadian theatre directors and writers had gained experience in community theatres across the country, and had been educated at Canadian colleges or universities. Eager for new experience, they travelled to the United States, Britain and Europe, studying and working in revolutionary theatres, from Jerzy Grotowski's Polish Laboratory Theatre in Warsaw, to Roger Planchon's company in Lyon, to the Living Theatre and Open Theatre in New York City. As these young Canadians returned home, they found Toronto ready for change, though most Torontonians hadn't noticed it yet. The new stages, acting companies and plays they were about to create would change Toronto theatre, and those changes would spread across the country, from Halifax to Vancouver.

CHAPTER ONE

Busted: Theatre Passe Muraille at Rochdale

On Wednesday, March 5, 1969, the day the Theatre Passe Muraille production of *Futz* was scheduled to open, producer William (Bill) Marshall challenged his city: 'We want to see what you can put on in Toronto.' The *Toronto Star* printed a rousing article, '*Futz* Brings Nudity, Bestiality to Toronto Stage.'

The Toronto Police showed little interest: 'If all it's got to show is a couple of bare mammary glands,' declared a spokesman, 'I don't think we'd even bother with it.' Marshall's producing partners, lawyers Miles O'Reilly and Arthur Pennington, invited crown counsel Peter Rickaby to the opening night. Rickaby was both the complainant and prosecutor in the 1965 obscenity conviction of art gallery owner Dorothy Cameron, still a scandal in Toronto. At the Central Library Theatre, a Toronto Police morality-squad plainclothes officer asked Rickaby if, in his opinion, an obscenity charge should be laid. 'It would be laughed out of court,' Rickaby told him.

Hours before the opening, the *Futz* company stage manager telephoned his actors with a warning that the police might charge them right after the performance. To avoid running into any law officers after the opening, the actors made their exit via the theatre's fire escape. On Thursday, March 6, after the second night's performance, the Toronto Police preferred charges of 'staging an indecent performance' and the following day legal summonses were issued to the director Jim Garrard, the three producers, the actors, the stage

Actresses Gina Laight, Bernice Gai Hune and Shoshana Brown.
Jim Garrard (right) directing *Futz* by Rochelle Owens
in the 'Zeus Suite' at Rochdale College, 1969.
Photo by Lionel Douglas, courtesy of R. Nasmith Archives.

crew and even the Central Library's teenage coatroom attendant.

As the play's scheduled three-week run proceeded, new summonses were issued to everyone after each night's presentation, each performance constituting a new offence under the law. The daily legal ceremony was covered by press and television, a major media event. The publicity put ticket sales through the roof; the producers scheduled additional performances, and invited the surprised American playwright, Rochelle Owens, to Toronto for interviews. Her rather 'Manhattan' comment was, 'This couldn't happen in New York. All this prurient sex. It's very corny.' Torontonians, who weren't offended by 'an indecent performance', as the warrants read, or by the denial of free speech, were unhappy with the rather provincial character of the entire affair. The *Toronto Telegram* commented, 'The press, the police, and those responsible for the production have this much in common: they have all become excited by a trace of smut.'

Jim Garrard at Rochdale, 1969. Photo by Robert Nasmith.

After its scheduled three-week run, *Futz* closed, as another theatre had previously reserved the Central Library. There was talk of moving the production to a new location, but this was just not possible. Passe Muraille had no production funds, the Trio partners were facing three weeks of Criminal Code charges and lawyers Pennington and O'Reilly, if convicted, could face sanctions by the Ontario Bar. The *Futz* arrests and the explosive media coverage they received produced extraordinary public exposure for the new Toronto theatre scene and energized local stage professionals of all kinds. In retrospect, it's interesting to examine why members of the *Futz* company were arrested.

For Toronto in 1969, it may well be that the Passe Muraille production of *Futz* was an 'indecent' act. The first act of *An Evening with Futz*, as the Central Library performance was called, was based on improvisations that director Jim Garrard had created in his Rochdale

College theatre classes, and was designed to prepare the audience for Rochelle Owens's play. Theatregoers had to reach their seats by stepping over actors sprawled in the aisles. After warm-up exercises, the cast questioned the audience about their ideas on bestiality, sexuality and the play's reputation. Sexual jokes and skits were mixed with the Walt Disney animated short *Three Little Pigs* and other visual materials. A recording of the Beatles singing 'Why Don't We Do It in the Road' was played. One critic described this first act as 'an extended series of obscene songs and dreary old jokes'. According to most reports, the audience interrogations were foolish, the songs and jokes were juvenile. Garrard disliked this first act so much he usually remained in the theatre lobby, refusing to watch. Now Theatre Passe Muraille, the new company he had founded just one year earlier, was at risk and he was facing charges, with no resources to defend himself.

Born in 1939, Jim Garrard grew up near the small cities of Oshawa and St. Catharines, Ontario, just east and southwest of Toronto.

Unable to afford university, he studied for a teacher's degree and became the principal of a small rural elementary school near Welland, Ontario. After taking summer and correspondence courses at Queen's University in Kingston, he left his school in 1963 to study for a BA in English, drama and philosophy. Over his three years studying with Fred Euringer, head of the Queen's University Drama Department, Garrard took part in forty productions and came to a decision: he wanted to be a director. Applying to the London Academy of Music and Dramatic Art, known as LAMDA, he gained entrance to the two-year acting program in September 1966. Fired up by his new theatrical ambitions, Garrard found himself at the centre of English-language theatre in 1960s London, watching Sir Laurence Olivier's *Othello* at Britain's National Theatre, the groundbreaking Panic Theatre from France, or New York's La Mama Experimental Theatre Club. In 1967, La Mama was touring London, and Garrard attended a performance of their hit *Tom Paine* by Paul Foster. Nearly twenty years later, he remembered his reaction: 'It was completely different from anything I'd ever seen, a true ensemble piece. It had brilliant direction from Tom O'Horgan, a very fascinating style of play, lots of musical instruments, the use of bodies to create settings. I saw *Futz* at the Mercury Theatre Club by the same company with basically the same cast. I was really struck by this idea that a lot of really young energetic actors could get together and work together through the kind of ensemble techniques we admired at the time, and put on these shows that were very, very different. So I came back to Canada with the view in mind to starting a theatre like La Mama.'

In February 1968, Jim Garrard arrived back in Toronto, looking for an acting job or work as a director. He tried the National Theatre School, the Stratford Festival and other possibilities, without any luck. Then, Charlotte Holmes, the theatre contact at the Ontario Arts Council, suggested Garrard find an affiliation with a college and told him about Rochdale: 'It sounded fairly interesting and it gave me both a place to live and a place to work.' When he turned up at the Rochdale College office and asked if he could start a theatre workshop, Rochdale's 'educational planner', Dennis Lee, later a well-known poet and editor, advised Garrard to just 'put up a sign'.

Rochdale College was conceived as an eighteen-story, double-towered high-rise student residence by Campus Co-operative Residences Incorporated, an aggressive, ambitious and successful provider of co-operative student housing in Toronto. Founded in 1937, with just seven members, the Co-op grew to 450 members and occupied thirty houses by 1967. When he was still a teenager, in 1957, Howard Edelman became the president of Campus Co-op. By 1969, he'd developed a radical new plan, a student-owned residence in a downtown Toronto high-rise. As a junior lecturer at the University of Toronto's Victoria College, Dennis Lee organized a group of idealistic educators within the same Campus Co-op Education Committee. Rochdale

College was incorporated as an educational institution and granted legal college status by a special act of the Ontario Provincial Government in 1964. They changed Rochdale from an experiment in student housing to an experiment in alternative higher education. Rochdale College became Canada's first 'free university'. 'Rochdale' was chosen for the college's name in honour of a grocery co-operative founded in 1844, in Rochdale, Lancashire, England, by twenty-eight weavers, followers of the British co-op pioneer Robert Owen.

Until the new Bloor Street high-rise could accommodate students, six downtown Toronto houses were rented as the temporary site of Rochdale College. Courses and workshops reflected the interests and talents of both faculty and students; classes included Eastern philosophy, phenomenology, contemporary social problems, silk-screening, film, drama and music. The drama workshops were held in

Rochdale College, 1969. Photo by Robert Nasmith.

a church basement on Huron Street by professional actor Tony Parr, a friend of Dennis Lee and his wife, Donna.

In April 1968, Jim Garrard started his own theatre workshops, in an Avenue Road coach house, owned by Howard Edelman's brother. He made a twelve-page proposal to the Rochdale council, detailing the drama program he planned. When he was a student in England, Garrard's wife had read him a French story about a hero with the power to pass through stone walls. Now, he named his proposal Theatre Passe Muraille (TPM), calling for a theatre without walls, with no distinctions between actors and spectators, between 'inside' and 'outside' the theatre, between drama as one art form, music as another and dance as yet another. Theatre Passe Muraille reflected Rochdale College priorities, with a focus on experimental drama, as well as community and social research. The Rochdale Theatre Project would establish a Community Theatre, with an Educational Unit and a Performing Unit.

The objective, Garrard stated in his proposal, was 'to avoid the kind of isolation that generally accompanies high-rise living, and to bring about the kind of contact that community should provide.' The permanent resident company would include a managing director, nine actors and two technicians, assisted by three researchers with expertise in music, design and educational liaison. The actors would only work within the company, developing a trust and understanding that would allow them to act as human beings in the community as well as performers. Garrard suggested a collapsible, transportable, 'plastic theatre' stage for Rochdale's second-floor terrace, a performance space that would be both adaptable and flexible. The ensemble company would be idealistic and experimental, rejecting 'theatre as architecture' in favour of 'the experience that ought to be and can be theatre'. The first year's operation would have a budget of $128,500.

There were some who accused Garrard of using his planned Community Theatre and Educational Unit as a tactic to gain Rochdale

College support for his own professional theatre ambitions. However, Garrard wrote that Theatre Passe Muraille's three branches were to be 'employed only for the sake of convenience. They cannot exist in fact, for theatre as produced entertainment and theatre as education cannot be distinguished.' Society and theatre couldn't be separated for Garrard, neither could social experiment and theatrical experiment. With an explosion of media attention, the Rochdale College high-rise opened in September 1968, though a number of floors were still not approved for residents. Jim Garrard was named as a 'full-time resource person', as Rochdale referred to its faculty, and received a subsidy equal to half the rent of his large two-bedroom apartment, in exchange for his contributions to the Rochdale Theatre Project.

The full-colour Rochdale College Handbook described the planned theatre programs:

> There are two aspects to theatre at Rochdale, one of which is presently functioning because the minimum requirements for its existence are a place and the interests of a group of people; this is the Community Theatre. The other aspect, professional theatre and educational research, is at present in an embryonic state while fundraising and organizing are carried out.

Garrard moved his regular improvisational workshops into the large living room of his eighteenth-floor 'Zeus Suite' in the Rochdale building. Al Morgan, an American draft resister, joined Garrard in leading the theatre games, sensitivity training, psychological exercises, trust exercises, birth exercises and other workshops. With his long dark hair and beard, the tall, gaunt Garrard was the image of a 1960s counterculture Christ figure. Twenty years later, he remembered his intensity with some embarrassment: 'I didn't like that whole messianic approach, it seemed manipulative and it seemed cheap. But at the time, it was very useful and it sometimes had very beautiful results.'

Garrard and Morgan also set up a playwrights' workshop in the fall of 1968. Performances took place once or twice a week in the Rochdale basement parking garage. Al Morgan contributed $5000 personally to the program, the Ontario Arts Council added another $4000 for an educational project. As he requested in his original proposal, Garrard was expecting financial support from the college, but none came. Rochdale's finances were in crisis from the day it opened. Realizing that Garrard was not interested in an activist political theatre, Morgan withdrew his funding and left Passe Muraille. The company's improvisational workshops eventually became rehearsals for a new production of *Tom Paine*, the play Garrard had admired in London. Playwright Paul Foster's London agent was approached about the performance, but all North American rights had already been sold to a producer in New York. Hearing about the Rochdale rehearsals, he threatened legal action.

Garrard remembered telephoning playwright Paul Foster: 'It was quite odd. This play is all about Tom Paine and liberty and freedom … and I said: "What's going on here? We've got a bunch of people up here who want to do your production, we're doing a beautiful production, and we're getting lawyers' letters saying we've got to close it down. Is this consistent with the play that you've written?" He'd never met me before, but he said, "Jim, I'm an American and all Americans are tainted." And that was the end of his contribution.'

Unable to obtain the rights, Garrard was forced to limit his production of *Tom Paine* to one 'private' performance in Rochdale's underground parking garage in December of 1968. As he later remembered, 'We used probably sixteen or twenty (parking) bays. We painted those black, we brought in 220 Volt power, and it was played completely on the flat. People sat on the floor, and we used a couple of bays as the stage. So it was three-quarters round, there was a concrete back wall to it, and we had in that little space up to twenty-five actors. One of the La Mama techniques was to use bodies

Tom Paine by Paul Foster. Directed by Jim Garrard.
This photo from Martin Kinch restaging, 1969. Set by Miro Kinch.
With Michael J. Reynolds (left), Bernice Gai Hune (centre),
Len Sedun (face on hand) and Booth Savage (far right).
Photo by Lionel Douglas, courtesy of R. Nasmith Archives.

to construct scenery ... it was good, it was cheap ... they were all in leotards anyway, and they'd just put on a cloak or put on a hat. It was very simple, like child-play really ... like exuberant kids dressing up.'

Even though the original Theatre Passe Muraille company had very little experience of any kind in the theatre, Garrard recalled this first *Tom Paine* performance as 'one of the best productions I've ever been associated with' and 'the perfect kind of monument to the times'. In the warm counterculture radiance of the late 1960s, the obvious limitations of the *Tom Paine* production were forgotten in the audience's enthusiasm for the play's revolutionary subject and the performance's 'underground' location. *Toronto Star* critic Don Rubin, later the editor of the *Canadian Theatre Review*, wrote ten years after the performance:

I remember trying to find my way one rainy night through the incensed halls of Rochdale College to see a production of Paul Foster's off-Broadway hit *Tom Paine*. When I found the space, I was told by Jim Garrard, the director of the piece and the founder of the group that would eventually call itself Passe Muraille (Beyond the Walls), that they were having trouble getting production rights to the script. This, for all intents and purposes, on opening night. Nevertheless, the show went on, *Tom Paine* spoke out for human freedom and the modern phase of theatrical growth in Toronto was officially ushered in.

Attracted by the revolutionary message of *Tom Paine* and the atmosphere of Rochdale itself, a number of theatre professionals gathered around Jim Garrard. Another American draft resister, Frank Masi, arrived at Rochdale with his actress wife, Judith. Masi was a qualified technical designer, with the ability to invent amazing theatrical stage effects for Passe Muraille. After *Tom Paine*, he designed a number of other Garrard productions, and Judith Masi appeared in them. Another new arrival was Ron Terrill, a 24-year-old Belleville, Ontario, native, who had worked at George Luscombe's Toronto Workshop Productions as an administrator, and had recently joined Trio Productions as the new company's production coordinator. Terrill attended the single *Tom Paine* performance and became Theatre Passe Muraille's first general manager. In 1970, he became a major force in the Festival of Underground Theatre (FUT), a groundbreaking event in Toronto theatre history. Disappointed by the abrupt closing of *Tom Paine*, Garrard put another production into rehearsal at once. He picked the other play he'd seen La Mama perform in London, *Futz*, by American playwright Rochelle Owens. This time, performance rights were arranged well in advance, and workshops and rehearsals were again held in Garrard's Zeus Suite. As Passe Muraille's operating budget had already been spent, and the Rochdale College council was too distracted by public criticism, regular Toronto Police invasions and continual financial crisis to consider additional funding, new production investment was urgently required. Ron Terrill invited the three partners in Trio Productions to observe a *Futz* rehearsal. As usual, at least half the cast was absent, and the rehearsal was being held in the vault of an unoccupied bank on the main floor of the College. Members of the Mothers of Invention, rock star Frank Zappa's band, were playing along with the rehearsal. As Garrard later remembered the scene, 'All of the Mothers of Invention except for Frank Zappa were visiting the city ... Penny Gawn, who was in the cast of *Futz*, had found them in the (Rochdale health food) restaurant, chatted with them, and they came in. They had actually had experience in these funny theatre games that we were doing, so they came in. They were making these fences, rolling around on the floor, Cy was there with his pig — it was a pretty surreal production. It's a surreal play.'

Trio Productions was a recently formed company with three partners. William (Bill) Marshall was an advertising man and producer, who was later a founding partner in the Toronto film festival known as the Festival of Festivals, Arthur Pennington and Miles O'Reilly were both Toronto lawyers. Born in Glasgow, Scotland, Marshall emigrated to Oshawa, Ontario, as a teenager, and had already achieved financial success as a theatre producer, importing the off-Broadway hit *Fortune and Men's Eyes*, by Canadian playwright John Herbert, for a nearly four-month run in Toronto and Montreal, during the winter of 1967–68. Pennington and O'Reilly were involved in student theatre at the University of Toronto, then joined the Uniplayers, a very active amateur theatre at the Unitarian Church they both attended, along with Ron Terrill. In March 1968, with the Uniplayers, the two lawyers produced an evening of Theatre of the Absurd plays at the Colonnade Theatre, with Bill Marshall as one of the directors.

In August, the three partners formed Trio Productions, announced their first season and began to sell ticket subscriptions.

Their intention was neither nationalist nor political, they would produce new, slightly controversial plays, which had achieved a proven success in London or New York, but had not yet been seen by audiences in Toronto. The first Trio season began in September 1968, with three productions opening within one week at three Toronto theatres: *Black Comedy* at the Toronto Workshop, *Staircase* at the Colonnade Theatre and *Marat/Sade* at the church hall on Trinity Square. It was a very ambitious program, the reviews were not very favourable and the box-office revenues for all three productions were nowhere near Trio's requirements. In financial difficulties, the partnership was forced to reconsider their plans, and, when they came to see the *Futz* rehearsal, Trio hadn't produced a play in nearly six months. After losing money on their first three productions, they were still committed to produce two more plays for their subscribers. They dealt with one production by assigning their rights to produce [o]The Killing of Sister George to Theatre Toronto, in exchange for a guarantee of tickets for Trio subscribers. Providing financial backing for Passe Muraille's *Futz* would be much less expensive for Trio than producing their own play and, if the production was successful, there could be money to be made.

The *Futz* rehearsal the Trio partners watched might have been in complete disorder, but the play's reputation from successful productions in New York and London and its controversial story could produce strong public interest with minimal financial risk. As Bill Marshall told the Toronto press, 'That's the kind of play we wanted to do — a real troublemaker of a play — because other people aren't doing anything like it.' As Trio couldn't bring their subscribers to the College parking garage, they rented the Central Library Theatre, just six blocks from Rochdale, and the scene of Marshall's success with *Fortune and Men's Eyes*. As they neared the opening, the Trio partners worried about the still disorganized rehearsals and the difficulty of attracting an audience. On the day of the opening, Marshall said in an interview, 'It's a madhouse. These kids never seem to come to rehearsal on time and when they do show up they're reading their lines off little slips of paper. But, you know, the dress rehearsal looked more organized than any dress rehearsal we've ever had before.' Garrard recalled that the Trio partners threatened to close *Futz* down on the night before it opened, demanding script cuts he refused to allow at first: 'Finally we struck an agreement. I said we'd cut these four pieces, and they agreed they'd go the distance with us.... They then turned around and made the fuss themselves by sending out press releases saying this play is full of nudity and obscenity and you've got to get down here.'

Cast photo from *Tom Paine* by Paul Foster, directed by Jim Garrard. This image is from the Martin Kinch restaging, 1969. Photo by Lionel Douglas, courtesy of R. Nasmith Archives.

CHAPTER TWO

Theatre Passe Muraille in Court

Based on its script, *Futz* seems relatively inoffensive today, and like most avant-garde theatre, it's a very moral work. Rochelle Owens's play was first produced in a Minneapolis workshop in 1965. The leading character, a farmer named Cyrus Futz, enjoys a happy sexual relationship with his pet sow, Amanda, in an abstract Ozark rural area of middle America. The hypocritical morality of the local farming community is outraged by Cy and Amanda's pure, simple love; their raucous, offstage lovemaking was a feature of Tom O'Horgan's outrageous New York production. The dark side of the story is the forceful repression of young people's sexuality by obsolete social morality. A boy goes mad when he sees Cy and Amanda making love, murders the girl who flirted with him, even though he loves her, and is hanged by society. The town slut, jealous of Amanda, causes the death of Cy and his love. *Futz* was famous for its bestiality and nudity, even though the first occurred offstage and the nudity involved a brief view of the bare breast of an actress offering to suckle her condemned son before his execution, a symbol of a mother's grief.

The *Futz* case was heard in Ontario Provincial Court in June 1969, and became a front-page story in every Toronto newspaper. Charges had already been dropped against the cast and crew, but director Jim Garrard, and producers William Marshall, Arthur Pennington and Miles O'Reilly were all charged with staging an indecent performance. The Crown called just two witnesses, officers of the Toronto

Police morality squad, who testified that they found the play both obscene and offensive, describing the naked breast one actress displayed, an onstage simulated sexual performance involving two males and a female, and the noisy offstage sexual cries of the coupling farmer, Cy, and his sow.

Celebrated defence lawyer Julian Porter called a number of expert witnesses, who testified to the moral and artistic content of the play. *Toronto Star* critic Nathan Cohen described Rochelle Owens as 'a playwright of high moral and ethical ambitions, but of no talent.' A total of thirteen witnesses, including respected members of the Toronto community, among them two clergymen, all testified that the production presented by Trio Productions and Theatre Passe Muraille was neither offensive nor obscene, but complied completely with Toronto's current community and theatrical standards.

The presiding judge, Justice P.J. Bolsby, was considered a legal maverick, not that well-grounded in the law and prone to impatient outbursts with lawyers he considered 'too superior'. On the first day of the trial, after reading over the transcript of Jim Garrard's first act 'happening', Bolsby pronounced himself outraged by the vulgar language which he found there, even though he admitted he'd heard similar remarks made during informal Ontario court meetings. In his opinion, four-letter words had no place on any Toronto stage. He quoted one crude joke from the transcript, a playful exchange between Little Red Riding Hood and the Big Bad Wolf:

LITTLE RED RIDING HOOD: My, what big teeth you have, grandma.
BIG BAD WOLF: All the better to eat you with.
LITTLE RED RIDING HOOD: Eat, eat, eat. Doesn't anyone fuck anymore?

This dialogue, Bolsby stated, was 'hopelessly vulgar, irrelevant, distasteful, and objectionable'. Despite testimony from various defence witnesses that the play's dialogue was no more obscene than most casual schoolyard conversation, the judge was not impressed: 'There's freedom of expression, but does it have to be done in the language of the barnyard or the barroom? Do we have to have vulgarisms hurled down our throat because of freedom of expression?' During the questioning of witnesses by the defence, and during Julian Porter's defence summation, Justice Bolsby interrupted to express his anxieties about coarse language used, and his annoyance that no expert witnesses had been called by the Crown to counter the defence experts. He even seemed puzzled by the obvious sincerity of the defence witnesses.

In his verdict, the Justice dismissed all the expert testimony for the defence as irrelevant, because the definition of obscenity under the Criminal Code referred to community standards, not expert ones: 'I do pay respect to their special knowledge. But, if left to my own devices, I could not see in it what they say is there.' Justice Bolsby held one matter as legally essential: 'People of this country do not wish the private intimacies between man and woman portrayed for the public view, any more than the people of this country want to peer into the bedrooms of the nation. There remains, as I sense it, a desire to retain an overall climate of decency in which we may live as social creatures and raise and develop and educate children. This does not mean knowledge and information should be suppressed. But we do not have absolute license and we do not seek to acquire licentiousness.' Director Garrard, and producers Marshall, Pennington, and O'Reilly were all found guilty of staging an indecent performance and fined a total $1,300.

Justice Bolsby's verdict was not a popular one, the Toronto media worried publicly over this latest attack on freedom of expression, as well as the damage to the city's reputation as a centre of at least marginal sophistication. The *Toronto Star* presented its editorial page comment on the trial as a theatre review of a play entitled The Damnation of *Futz*:

What The Damnation of *Futz* lacks in originality it makes up for with a Chaplinesque, deadpan humour that is nicely sustained from start to finish. Only occasionally are there lapses into slapstick comedy, as when a defence witness says that *Futz* can't be all that bad when a local movie house is showing an even racier epic called *Can Hieronymous Merkin Ever Forget Mercy Humpe and Find True Happiness?*

Like Batman and Robin at the mere mention of crime in Gotham city, the police scribble down an approximation of the movie title and race off to defend Virtue in Toronto. Sure enough, the movie is as obscene as they said it was — at least, the police think so — and the operators and distributing companies are promptly issued with summonses. It looks like a clean sweep for Virtue until we come to the punchline; *Hieronymous Merkin* had already been approved for viewing by the Ontario Board of Censors. What happens now? If the distributors are just as responsible as the exhibitors, must the police also lay charges against the censor? The comic possibilities are endless.

The *Star* editorial ended with a deconstruction of the legal concept of obscenity, as it was applied to the *Futz* case:

What remains to be shown is how anyone can be corrupted by a book, a movie or a play who wasn't corrupt before. In the case of a four-letter word, for example, only two things are possible: Either the listener hasn't heard the word before — in which case it is meaningless to him — or he knows it — in which case he is already corrupt. Even with something as demonstrably outlandish as *Futz*, would anyone believe that depraved theatre-goers are suddenly going to start flocking to the countryside? That no pig will be safe in its sty?

Ridiculous, yes. But no more ridiculous than the idea that a judge, censor, minister, or detective can presume to know the meaning of obscenity or to know the 'prevailing opinion' about something as intimate as personal morality. Who knows? Perhaps closing down theatres is more obscene than anything that goes on inside them. Whatever the case, Toronto's new comedy deserves to be laughed out of town.

Toronto newspapers had portrayed the '*Futz* Four' as victims of the over-eager Toronto Police and a conservative judge, an image which would soon be reinforced by the media circus surrounding the 'Chicago Seven Conspiracy Trial', later in 1969. The two Toronto Police morality-squad officers were represented as philistine fools, reading their testimony hesitantly from notes, Justice Bolsby was portrayed as foolishly incredulous of the well-considered moral positions very clearly presented by critics Nathan Cohen and Robert Fulford. But the Toronto media were missing a very important aspect of the *Futz* case. Toronto's rapid growth, its replacement of Montreal as Canada's largest city and the country's financial capital, brought with it metropolitan problems like strip clubs and sex parlours, drug sales and street crime and, most disturbing of all, social revolution. The generational rebellion that gave birth to both Rochdale College and Theatre Passe Muraille involved a direct challenge to the existing social structure, and it was a very natural reaction for the established society to strike back. In the *Futz* case, Canada's traditional freedom of expression forced Toronto society to battle rebellion by attacking four-letter words and bare breasts. Even though Justice Bolsby didn't ever read or see the play, he made his position very clear: 'Society isn't really the way the play depicts it.'

For Theatre Passe Muraille, the *Futz* bust and trial were obvious attacks on Rochdale as a radical social experiment. Jim Garrard saw it quite simply:

> What really bothered people was the idea that this guy slept with his pig, and the idea that we were saying something about the society we lived in. In Rochelle Owens' play everybody wanted to kill Cy Futz, they *do* kill him; and the only thing he does is he's in love with his pig Amanda. He lives quietly by himself, minding his own business on his farm, and everybody in society wanted to kill him.

> We felt that we were in a similar position. It's true. Everyone wanted to kill Rochdale, and they eventually did. They used all the powers of the police, the courts; everything.... Rochdale was a beautiful place. For all the violence that was there, there was also incredible gentleness and getting along together and fair-mindedness. It was a very beautiful place.

By the late 1960s, Rochdale's social rebellion was taking a more confrontational position. The College attracted radical thinkers from across North America and their avowed mission was to change society, in Canada or the United States. Jim Garrard's social theatre experiments attracted little attention when they were performed in the Rochdale parking garage, but once Trio Productions presented *Futz* at the Central Library Theatre, they were invading the establishment's territory. 'This is for the public,' Justice Bolsby ruled, 'not a group of intellectuals.' This invasion was the 'obscenity' for which he convicted the defendants.

In any urban centre, the theatre community performs to satisfy its audience, in the expectation that the audience will ultimately return the favour. Some Toronto artists were immediately aroused to support *Futz*, but most of the local theatre professionals were happier to look the other way. *Toronto Star* critic Nathan Cohen wrote about how disappointed he was with the lack of interest in Toronto's theatre community: 'Some groups have gone to considerable trouble to disassociate themselves from any possible connection with Trio Productions, Theatre Passe Muraille, or the production of plays which might incur police displeasure.' But these local theatre groups didn't seem to view censorship by the Toronto Police or the Ontario Crown Attorney as dangerous to their own freedom of expression, because the Rochdale Drama Project and its audience had little connection with them. As Jim Garrard remembered twenty years later: 'The existing theatrical community didn't regard us at the time as legitimate and serious theatre practitioners.'

Gerome Ragni (standing) and friends at Toronto's Convocation Hall, 1970.
Photo by Lionel Douglas, courtesy of R. Nasmith Archives.

But the Toronto theatre scene was about to change; if 1969 was the year of *Futz*, 1970 became the year of *Hair*.

The local production of the hit Broadway musical, with book and lyrics by Gerome Ragni and James Rado and music by Canadian Galt MacDermot, ran for a record-breaking year at the Royal Alex Theatre. Hailed by Toronto media and audiences, *Hair* brought rock music, hippies, four-letter words and nudity to the Toronto stage. As critic Nathan Cohen noted, 'It appears to embody all the trends and impulses of the late 1960s among disaffected youth. In point of fact, when you find society applauding and embracing a show that claims to be savaging it, you can be certain that its real revolutionary menace is non-existent.'

Even though the fines imposed on the *Futz* producers were not heavy, they were forced to appeal their guilty verdicts because lawyers Arthur Pennington and Miles O'Reilly could be disbarred if their Criminal Code convictions stood. The appeal of the *Futz* verdict began in March 1970, and the popular status of the Toronto production of *Hair* was a major argument for the defence. The Crown called the same two morality-squad officers as their sole witnesses. The defence argued that the community that could accept *Hair* as popular entertainment must also be able to accept *Futz*. There was more nudity in *Hair* and a similar amount of vulgarity, but, while Nathan Cohen had commented on Rochelle Owens's 'high moral and ethical ambitions', he noted that *Hair*'s success was due to the show's slick packaging of 'zeitgeist entertainment', a spectacle of wonderful talent with no ethical or moral pretensions. The defence invited Appeal Court Justice William Lyon to view a performance of *Hair*, to help him appreciate local community standards. Justice Lyon agreed, once tickets were also provided for a group of court officials, as well as Mrs Lyon.

In his April 1970 verdict, Lyon referred to the Supreme Court's finding that 'Tolerance is to be preferred to proscription' and ruled that *Futz* served no base purpose and that the dramatic impact of the play would be seriously impaired by removal of its sexual content. He reprimanded the morality-squad witnesses, recommending that police officers be made more aware of public acceptance of standards of taste or morality, and acquitted the four defendants, reversing their 1969 convictions. The Toronto arts community belatedly identified with the defendants and gloated over their delayed victory. Nathan Cohen hoped that 'the police may be effectively deterred, through Judge Lyon's decision, from laying charges of obscenity against theatrical presentations.' Within six years, he would be proven wrong, and Theatre Passe Muraille would be busted again.

The Crown decided not to appeal the acquittals. The three Trio partners had promised Jim Garrard that they would cover his legal costs and they kept their word.

During the year that followed the *Futz* bust, Jim Garrard had little time for Theatre Passe Muraille, but he was deeply involved with the doomed battle to save Rochdale College. 'As the problems became more mundane,' he remembered, 'we looked for more romantic decisions.' Garrard led a fundraising drive, which became notorious for selling degrees by mail. He became 'King of Rochdale' after suggesting at a boring committee meeting that monarchy was a more effective form of government than democracy. He wore his regal robes to Rochdale public events, amusing the media and his fans, allowing loyal retainers to kiss his royal ring. After his April 1970 acquittal, the exhausted Garrard accepted an artist-in-residence appointment at Simon Fraser University in British Columbia. William Marshall became the manager of David Crombie's successful campaign to become the Mayor of Toronto. Arthur Pennington and Miles O'Reilly returned to their law practices, avoiding professional theatre in the future.

The last of the genuine 1960s counterculture idealists lived out the Rochdale experiment's final years in the decaying twin towers. Swamped by economic and legal entanglements, the building was seized in 1973 by its mortgagor, the Central Mortgage and Housing Corporation, and sold to Metro Toronto in 1976. The last tenants were evicted in 1975, then the towers were re-opened as government-assisted housing for senior and handicapped citizens in 1980, though the name Rochdale was no longer used.

Eleven years earlier, Theatre Passe Muraille had already moved to a new home. As news of the *Futz* company being charged broke in March 1969, Trio Productions received an unexpected offer from Jim Fisk, rector of the Church of the Holy Trinity in downtown Toronto. Fisk deeply resented the police censorship of *Futz*, and was very vocal in his support for the production; he was one of two clergymen who would testify at both trials. Just across the street from Fisk's church, at 11 Trinity Square, was the parish hall, which had been occupied by a number of Toronto theatrical productions, including Trio's 1968 *Marat/Sade*. Now the rector offered the building as a new location for *Futz*, with a monthly rental of just $500. In spite of Rochdale College's increasing fiscal problems, the governing council, of which Jim Garrard was now a member, voted to pay Passe Muraille's rent. Garrard was impressed by what he found at the parish hall: a large open room, some sixty by forty feet, with a high ceiling and excellent acoustics, two offices at the far end, and a meeting room above them. This was the flexible performance venue he had imagined creating at Rochdale, the ideal 'empty space' that revolutionary British director Peter Brook talked about. This perfect venue for Theatre Passe Muraille was just a block from the Yonge Street entertainment strip, home of jazz and rock clubs–joint centre, with Yorkville, of the 1960s Toronto music scene. A reasonable walk away were the established Royal Alexandra Theatre, the O'Keefe Centre, and the still-under-construction St. Lawrence Centre civic theatre.

The Church of the Holy Trinity was completed in 1847, financed by the legacy of an Anglican minister's wife, who'd been most impressed by one of Ontario Bishop John Strachan's English preaching tours. Her anonymous donation of 5,000 pounds for the building of a church in the Toronto diocese had just two conditions, that it be dedicated to the Holy Trinity and that its pews be available to all comers at no charge. The Hon. John Simcoe Macaulay, son of the personal physician to Upper Canada Governor Lord Simcoe, donated land from his family estate along Yonge Street as the site of the church. The parish hall was built in 1888, on the southeast corner of Trinity Square, opposite the church. Until 1930, the hall was occupied by a parochial school and a Sunday school; it then became a hostel for unemployed men during the Depression, and a servicemen's lodge during World War II. From the 1940s to the late 1950s, the hall was rented by a local radio station as a studio for live drama broadcasts.

When Jim Fisk took over as rector in 1962, he reclaimed the church hall and turned it over to social programs. With its longstanding social tradition, the Church of the Holy Trinity became a natural focus for the growing street activity in Toronto's downtown. For Jim Fisk, the Trinity Square parish hall seemed an ideal location for Theatre Passe Muraille.

UBU Raw. Directed by Paul Thompson. Festival of Underground Theatre, 1970. Left to right: Paul Thompson, Bob Dermer, unknown actor with back to us. Photo by Lionel Douglas, courtesy of R. Nasmith Archives.

UBU Raw. Directed by Paul Thompson. Festival of Underground Theatre, 1970. That is Bob Dermer with his head through the windshield; Dini Baker in front of him; and Don Steinhouse behind the wheel. Photo by Lionel Douglas, courtesy of R. Nasmith Archives.

UBU Raw. Directed by Paul Thompson, 1970. With Don Steinhouse (bending over), Dini Baker, Bob Dermer and unknown actors. Photo by Lionel Douglas, courtesy of R. Nasmith Archives.

CHAPTER THREE

Passe Muraille at Trinity Square, Part One

Holy Trinity's ministry traditionally included theatre; a celebrated *Christmas Story* had been performed every year since 1937 and an Easter play was usually included as well. In the 1960s, the hall was home to the Religion and Theatre Council and rented to various independent theatre productions. After Trio's *Marat/Sade* closed, Theatre Toronto occupied the building until it was dissolved. Theatre Passe Muraille moved to Trinity Square on May 1, 1969. The first event it held was a benefit dance on June 23, publicized as a 'huge free-form happening', which raised over $2,500 for the *Futz* defence fund. On the next weekend performances began; part of a street festival organized by Trinity Church, the actors were members of a visiting college group from Ann Arbor, Michigan, who called themselves A Company. Led by expatriate Newfoundlander Chris Brookes, who later returned home to found the Mummers Troupe, A Company remained at Trinity Square all summer, producing three original plays by company member Jeff Levy: *Portrait, Itch* and *Nightmare with Hat*, as well as Samuel Beckett's *Endgame* and Sam Shepard's *Forensic and the Navigators.* Garrard remembered some disagreements between A Company and Passe Muraille: 'They thought we were too sloppy, and we thought they were too humourless.' Relations were not enhanced when Brookes's group cut a hole through the floor for one production.

During the summer of 1969, the parish hall was known as Theatre 11, and was home to a growing number of independent, low-budget productions, sharing resources and expertise with Passe Muraille. As Jim Garrard reported to the Ontario Arts Council at the end of the summer: 'Our major productions were *Balls* (Paul Foster), *Home Free* (Lanford Wilson), and *An evening with The Maids* (Jean Genet). Other productions were *The Marriage Proposal* (Chekhov), *New Step* (Leonard Cohen), *Escurial* (Michel de Ghelderode). In addition, we were responsible for the production of several plays by persons involved in our theatre drop-in centre at Trinity Square. These included *Santa Claus* (ee cummings), *The Babies* (Anna Lippman), *Project X* (Philip Hopcraft), *The Laundromat Special* (Group) and four weeks of rehearsal for *The Beard* (Michael McClure).'

A notable event of the summer was Garrard's production of Genet's *The Maids*, which he entitled *An evening with The Maids* (as he had *Futz*), and introduced with an opening act set in a sleazy sailors' bar in Marseille, with a midnight drag show version of the play, waiters in gold jockstraps, the young Kate Nelligan (then known as Trish) as a French floozie, and composer Phil Schreibman, who had written songs for *Tom Paine* and *Futz*, improvising a live score on the piano. Passe Muraille also became a very busy theatre 'drop-in' centre that summer of 1969, as Garrard reported to the OAC:

> For a number of reasons, mostly financial, we saw fit to open our doors to anyone who showed interest, good intentions, and could fit in with the existing group. By the end of July, we had over forty people working more or less regularly on theatre things at Trinity. Many of these people were untrained. Only twelve were being paid.... Here were a group of people of very diverse theatrical experience, many of whom would normally be more properly found on the audience side of things, joining together to solve theatrical problems for themselves.

Garrard's report was written as a plea for financing from the Ontario Arts Council, outlining Passe Muraille's one-year history and planned future activities. He felt the first summer at Trinity Square had slowed the theatre's growth as a professional company.

Plans for the 1969–70 season included a reduction in community and educational activities, an increase in artistic explorations, and more productions developed from them. 'This does not reflect dissatisfaction with our accomplishments during the last year' he wrote, 'but we are looking for excellence. And a much leaner operation is necessary.' Garrard doesn't seem to have realized how the move from Rochdale's social reform theoretics to Trinity Square's downtown street scene was already changing his theatre. As actor Booth Savage remembered later, 'You didn't go there to see plays, so much as to find out what was going on.' Garrard was always a conceptualist; Passe Muraille was now becoming a practical theatre. In the fall of 1969, new directors were being attracted by Passe Muraille's accessibility and reputation.

Hoping to build his company talent pool, Garrard recruited a new group of actors through the Canadian Theatre Centre referral service, and asked twenty-six-year-old Martin Kinch, theatre consultant with the Central Ontario Drama League, to help him stage productions. Having just spent the summer in Stratford, directing a new company he'd started with co-director John Palmer, Kinch also invited Palmer to Passe Muraille. They were soon joined by Kinch's friend Paul Thompson as technical director and stage manager. Kinch and Palmer brought their own theatrical ambition and developing showmanship to Passe Muraille, and very soon overshadowed Garrard's more intellectual approach. Paul Thompson's limited experience and reputation kept him in an inferior technical position for the time being, though he would eventually take his place as a company director.

Martin Kinch was born in London, England, in 1943, and emigrated to Canada with his family in 1948. At high school in London, Ontario, the teenager was involved in theatre, then joined the local amateur company, the London Little Theatre, where his mother was also a member. He received an honours degree in English Literature at the University of Western Ontario, where, in 1965, he directed Genet's *Deathwatch*, which won him a prize at the Canadian Universities Drama League Festival in Montreal. There, Kinch first met playwright and director John Palmer, a student at Carleton University in Ottawa. During that summer, Kinch directed Genet's *The Balcony* at fellow University of Western Ontario student Keith Turnbull's operation, Summer Theatre '65, in the Oasis Restaurant Theatre, a rented downtown-London strip club. The next year, when Turnbull produced Summer Theatre '66 with only Canadian plays, Kinch and Paul Thompson co-directed *Marise*, by Jack Cunningham.

Now a university graduate, Kinch found a job as an insurance adjuster in Toronto, but soon realized that a life without theatre was not for him. He submitted his application to a new young directors program, recently organized by George Merten of the Youth and Recreation Branch of the Ontario Department of Education, supported by Charlotte Holmes, of the Ontario Arts Council, and Tom Hendry, of the Canadian Theatre Centre. A group of experts in Toronto would select a group of young Ontario theatre directors for the Directors Training in Britain program. Successful candidates would be sent to apprentice for one-year terms with established British theatre companies. They would then return to Ontario, to be employed as travelling directors for amateur community theatres. Both Martin Kinch and John Palmer were selected for training, Palmer at the Citizens' Theatre in Glasgow; Kinch went to the Birmingham Repertory Theatre with his wife, Miro, who was attending the School of Theatre Design at Birmingham's College of Art.

At the Birmingham Rep, Kinch was assigned to manage a new program of late-night experimental productions. As part of this series, he directed Samuel Beckett's *Endgame*, Jean-Claude van Itallie's

War, Olwen Wymark's *Lunchtime Concert* and one act of *Daily News from the Whole World* by Rae Davis, with whom he'd worked in London, Ontario. During their year in England, the Kinchs were in regular contact with John Palmer, who telephoned and visited them from Glasgow. Jim Garrard was also in England in 1967, studying at LAMDA in London, where he met with both Kinch and Palmer. Martin and Miro Kinch returned to Canada, following their year in Birmingham. Fulfilling his commitment to the Directors Training in England program, Kinch was employed by the Central Ontario Drama League as a travelling director for its member clubs. During the winter of 1968–69, Kinch directed Jerome Lawrence's *Inherit the Wind* in Oshawa and Luigi Pirandello's *Right You Are If You Say You Are* in Etobicoke.

During that same winter, Theatre Passe Muraille was producing *Tom Paine* at Rochdale, and *Futz* at the Central Library. Radical theatre was 'happening' in Toronto. In June 1969, as the first *Futz* trial was being heard, Kinch directed *Plague ... So Far* at Toronto's Central YMCA, an actors' collective work based on Daniel Defoe's *A Journal of the Plague Year*, with added twentieth-century references. Jim Garrard greatly admired the production. As the *Plague* show closed, the Kinchs left for Stratford, Ontario, to join John Palmer at their new storefront operation, Canadian Place Theatre.

John Palmer was born in 1943, in Sydney, Nova Scotia, but grew up in Ottawa, Ontario. He began acting as a teenager, at school and at the Ottawa Little Theatre. He spent a year in pre-med studies at Queen's University, then enrolled in English Literature at Carleton University. With other future theatre professionals, including actor Saul Rubinek, playwright Larry Kardish and director Timothy Bond, he joined Carleton's Sock and Buskin drama club, where he could explore his own absurdist and non-realist ambitions as a playwright and director. At the 1965 Canadian Universities Drama League Festival in Montreal, where he met Martin Kinch, Palmer's play *Visions of an*

Unseemly Youth, won the award for Best Original Play. The following year, the CUDL Festival was held in Toronto and Palmer's production of Larry Kardish's play *Goebbels Gobbledygook* won awards for Best Production, Best Direction and Best Original Play. In the spring of 1966, *Goebbels* was revived at Toronto's Colonnade Theatre and also invited to a theatre festival at Yale University.

After graduating from Carleton University in 1966, Palmer decided on a theatre career, writing to a selection of professional Canadian companies, offering his services.

A few theatres rejected his offer, most didn't even bother. Palmer was furious at this; he was being denied employment in his own country, by foreign artistic directors. As he remembered: 'The reason I couldn't get a job was because I was Canadian. The theatres were run by Brits, and they were bringing over more Brits ... I thought, well, this has got to change.'

Without any theatre work in 1966, Palmer and his friends from Carleton University organized their own company to produce plays at Ottawa's famous coffee house Le Hibou, where the owner scheduled their performances between bookings for his regular musical acts. The company rehearsed in an unheated upstairs room, and scheduled a series of plays, including *The Seagull, Woyzeck, The Knack, Entertaining Mr Sloane*, and *The Duchess of Malfi*, each production running for three nights per week for three weeks. At the end of the Ottawa season, Palmer announced the company would travel to Stratford, to perform in competition with the Stratford Festival: 'If we're going to change the country, we've got to go to Stratford.' A university professor, whose wife acted with the company, loaned them $1,000 and a station wagon. They all drove to Stratford, rented a house and persuaded Harry Finlay, owner of the Black Swan, the local coffee house, to let them perform between his regular musical acts, as they had at Le Hibou.

The company was renamed the New Vic Theatre for its 1967 summer in Stratford. They performed two plays by Palmer, *Visions of an Unseemly Youth* and *Confessions of a Necrophile, or Never Laugh When a Hearse Goes By*, and Saul Rubinek's one-man show, *Diary of a Madman*, adapted from the Nikolai Gogol story. The fourth scheduled play, *Occasional Seasoning* by Larry Kardish, wasn't produced until Palmer came back to Stratford two years later, with the Canadian Place Theatre.

The New Vic performances played to very small audiences, frequently less than five, but the season did attract some of the most influential people in Canadian theatre. One night, Palmer was startled to realize that *Toronto Star* critic Nathan Cohen and his family were the entire audience for the performance of Saul Rubinek's *Diary of a Madman*. After the show, Palmer jumped onto the stage to offer the surprised Cohen family another play. Cohen's review wasn't positive, but he did admire the company's nerve: 'There is a nucleus here of something theatrically alive and perhaps eloquent, an organization that might deserve a future.' The founder of the Shaw Festival, Brian Doherty, invited the New Vic company to perform on the Festival stage in Niagara-on-the-Lake, on the Shaw company's day off. Palmer staged his two plays on the set of *Major Barbara*, after demanding that all the elegant period furniture be hung from the walls or stacked in front of the doors.

During his 1967 summer at Stratford, Palmer maintained his growing reputation as the enfant terrible of the Canadian stage. Stratford star Alan Bates was refused admission to a New Vic performance by Palmer because he was late, and Palmer once burst into Stratford artistic director Jean Gascon's office, demanding to direct a play on the Festival stage. He was disappointed that the Stratford management barely seemed to notice him: 'I could have been co-opted very easily,' he remembered much later. During the Glasgow Citizens' Theatre's 1967–68 season, apprentice director Palmer was put in charge of the experimental stage, the Close Theatre Club, where he directed plays by Eugene Ionesco and Jules Feiffer. Although both

Saul Rubinek in *Spring Awakening* by Frank Wedekind.
Directed by Martin Kinch, 1970.
Photo by Lionel Douglas, courtesy of R. Nasmith Archives.

Palmer and Martin Kinch remembered learning a great deal about directing techniques, organization and craft during their year in Britain, neither was very impressed by the quality of theatre they saw there, in London or at the regional theatres. Palmer remembers he was even more determined to work at the top level in Canada, 'because you came back realizing you were as good as anybody else.' He returned to Canada in the fall of 1968, after travelling in Europe with Saul Rubinek, and went to Woodstock, Ontario, as director of the Woodstock Little Theatre there.

The Woodstock Little Theatre soon became a focus for unhappy local youth and for Palmer's own battle against the Canadian theatre establishment. For him, the national Little Theatre tradition was the enemy of his own theatrical ambitions, and its crowning annual event, the Dominion Drama Festival, was outright theatrical colonialism, continuing a British theatre style made antique fifteen years earlier by John Osborne's *Look Back in Anger.* Palmer attacked with an energetic and imaginative production of *Tango* by Polish playwright Slavomir Mrozek, which was judged the best production at the 1969 Ontario regional festival. The Woodstock Little Theatre was overjoyed when its production was selected to represent Ontario at the national Dominion Drama Festival competition in Kelowna, BC. There, Palmer's *Tango* sparked a controversy which attracted national media coverage and a scandal which rocked the top DDF management.

On the night of the performance, a very upscale audience arrived at the six-hundred-seat Kelowna Community Theatre to find giant lengths of plastic tubing draped across the front steps, banner-waving youths shouting slogans from the roof, and assorted piles of junk heaped in the lobby. In the theatre, every seat was already occupied by an inflated plastic garbage bag; on the stage, televisions tuned to local stations were aimed at the arriving audience, already confused about where to sit. The production was also wildly unconventional, as the Canadian Press reported: 'The three hours of just about every modern theatrical idea in the book included flashing lights, a go-go band and a brief topless appearance by Elaine Reed, her back to the dwindling audience....' The next morning, Palmer was summoned to a dressing-down by a stern Pauline McGibbon, former president of the DDF and later lieutenant-governor of Ontario. The Woodstock Little Theatre, which had cheered Palmer's Ontario victory with *Tango*, was deeply embarrassed by the scandal in Kelowna. Palmer agreed not to return for a second season.

He returned to Toronto to meet with his friend Martin Kinch. During their time in Britain, they had realized they both had similar ideas about theatre aesthetics and politics. With the Edinburgh Festival as a model, they decided to produce a 'fringe festival' during the

1969 Stratford season, by producing new Canadian plays in an unconventional theatre space, just as Palmer had done two years earlier. They rented a vacant dry goods store opposite the Festival's Avon Theatre, installing a simple thrust stage with seating for about sixty people. Naming their new company the Canadian Place Theatre, after the off-off-Broadway American Place Theatre, they gathered actors from Palmer's Ottawa and Woodstock groups, from Kinch's productions in central Ontario, and added a few local Stratford actors.

Company members lived communally in a rented house and were paid seven dollars per week, very irregularly. The group usually ate dinner at the Black Swan coffee house, where owner Harry Finlay's daily communal meal for summer gypsies had become a Stratford tradition. They interrupted marathon rehearsal sessions by smashing empty coke bottles against an upstairs 'bouncing wall', as 'primal therapy'. The first productions, *Occasional Seasoning* by Larry Kardish and *The Dance* by Terry Cox, both directed by John Palmer, began, in repertory, in July. Two works by John Palmer, directed by Martin Kinch, *Memories for My Brother* and *Anthem*, opened in August, provoking complaints from the Stratford Police. As well as the taped personal histories of its actors, *Anthem* included some nudity, and the Canadian Place producers were warned to close their play, immediately. An appeal was made to the Stratford Festival literary manager, playwright Tom Hendry, co-author of the controversial Festival musical *Satyricon*, which was currently playing across the street at the Avon Theatre.

Hendry met with Kinch and Palmer to discuss the possible police action. He had found their Canadian Place operation an exciting alternative to the more staid Festival establishment, and also shared fellow playwright Palmer's desire to see Canadian plays on Canadian stages. On July 9, 1969, *Toronto Star* theatre critic Don Rubin gave the Larry Kardish play *Occasional Seasoning* a very negative review, but he also wrote:

Yet, for all this negativism, I have the distinct feeling that Canadian Place Theatre may yet make a real contribution to Canadian playwriting. Its people are serious and its intentions honourable. Such a combination offers real possibility....

Most reactions to Canadian Place in the summer of 1969 were similar, whatever the limitations of the productions staged, the goal of producing new Canadian plays made the season a turning point. Along with Jim Garrard, Martin Kinch and John Palmer were now considered to be the principal directors of the new Toronto theatre.

In September 1969, the three came together in Toronto. Preoccupied with the continuing problems of Rochdale College, Garrard looked forward to Kinch's help at Passe Muraille. He, Palmer and Kinch, often at odds with each other, had ended their Stratford summer with a fistfight, but both came to Trinity Square, along with Edna Widenmaier from the Canadian Place company. She became secretary to both Kinch and Garrard, as well as secretary to the New Directors Group they founded later that winter.

The first autumn production scheduled at Passe Muraille was a remount of *Tom Paine*, with the rights pre-arranged this time. Kinch was supervising the rehearsals, but he had some difficulty communicating Garrard's direction to the company; Kinch seemed to feel Passe Muraille's founder was a kind of absent deity. Rehearsals went very slowly, and the first play of the season became Palmer's new production of *Memories for My Brother, Part 1*, which opened on November 4, 1969, for a two-week run. Palmer left for Ottawa soon after, intending to focus on writing, and *Tom Paine* opened for a five-week run on November 20. The designer of both plays was Miro Kinch, who would be a regular designer in the new Toronto theatre scene. Theatre Passe Muraille was now re-confirmed as a theatrical production company, but neither play was greeted with critical or popular success. *Globe and Mail* critic Herbert Whittaker took Miro Kinch to task for her

Memories scaffolding set: 'Nude Memories swing about jungle gym.' He had kinder words for the author: 'Palmer writes sensitively, poetically, and entertainingly, although not always at the same time.'

The *Toronto Star*'s Nathan Cohen wanted more from the new theatre: 'Like Rochdale College, where it originated and to which it is still affiliated, Theatre Passe Muraille has a laudable desire to break free of traditional and sterile practices. It wants to be relevant in form and content, to stir theatre-goers to new perceptions and considerations. Such intentions are honourable. But it will have to do infinitely better if it is to establish a real place for itself and exert any influence.' In December 1969, Passe Muraille faced a new economic crisis. The fifth administrative director had just left and the theatre had no functioning financial organization, as its cheques began to bounce.

Shain Jaffe, a young American with a business background, had emigrated to Canada to escape the draft. Jaffe set up a basic accounting system, instructing Edna Widenmaier and Paul Thompson how to use it. Garrard resigned as artistic director, dedicating himself to fundraising for Passe Muraille and Rochdale. Martin Kinch, already rehearsing his production of *Richard III*, would be the new artistic director. Kinch cancelled his production, reduced the acting company by two-thirds and cut all salaries. This *Richard III* might have been very interesting; actress Bernice Gai Hune rehearsed playing Richard's hump, hanging on the actor's shoulder. Charlotte Holmes of the Ontario Arts Council arranged an emergency grant, but it was obvious that Passe Muraille couldn't survive long without a popular audience success. Kinch decided on a double bill of two one-act plays, *Sweet Eros* by Terrence McNally and *In His Own Write* by John Lennon, Victor Spinetti and Adrienne Kennedy.

Delayed by budget problems, the production didn't open until late January 1970, enjoying rave reviews and soldout houses. Ticket sales were encouraged by the seductive, sexual nudity that was an essential element of *Sweet Eros*, the tale of a shy young man who abducts the young girl he desires. Actress Margaret Keith was bound to a chair, facing upstage, as her kidnapper stripped her scene by scene, leaving her naked at the play's climax. 'New audiences' were attracted to Passe Muraille; the first rows were packed with men who normally passed their time in the strip clubs and sex movie theatres on nearby Yonge Street. Attendance was also increased by John Lennon and Yoko Ono's celebrated 'bed-in' for peace, which had made headlines in Montreal the previous summer. The double bill ran for seven weeks, then went on tour to York and Brock Universities. Passe Muraille had produced an audience success that matched *Futz* and survived.

On March 26, Passe Muraille actor Ashleigh Moorhouse opened John Osborne's *A Bond Honoured*, which he directed and helped to finance. Three of the new Toronto theatre's best actors, Clare Coulter, Booth Savage and Don Steinhouse, were matched with three of the worst, Martin Kinch, Shain Jaffe and Paul Thompson. The production

A Bond Honoured by John Osborne. Directed by Ashleigh Moorhouse, 1970. With Martin Kinch (back to us), Paul Thompson, Clare Coulter and Don Steinhouse.
Photo by Lionel Douglas, courtesy of R. Nasmith Archives.

was an acknowledged disaster, by the critics, the very meagre audiences and the actors themselves. Booth Savage hated *A Bond Honoured* so much that he put a sign on the theatre door one night, telling the audience that the performance was cancelled; fewer than ten people showed up on many nights. Nathan Cohen wrote a negative review:

> Conceivably, the production is meant to satirize the excesses of Renaissance melodrama and Osbornian vehemence. But this attributes to the director and his players a sense of design and intelligence unwarranted by their observable actions. Like the play, the show is both a tragedy and a farce, but for all the wrong causes.

Cohen bellowed in anger as he left the theatre, slamming the wall with his cane.

The Passe Muraille season ended with two Canadian plays, neither of which had any more success than the Osborne play, with critics or audiences. The first to open was *Notes from Quebec*, adapted by Paul Thompson from Jean-Claude Germain's play *Diguidi, Diguidi, Ha! Ha! Ha!* This production is important for two reasons; it was the first play Paul Thompson directed at Passe Muraille, and it led to actress Clare Coulter's decision to focus on small theatres. In a 1975 interview, she remembered: 'When I first started out, I used to have all my sights trained on big audiences and big theatres. But I adjusted to that after coming to Passe Muraille.'

Then on May 27, *The Hanging of William O'Donnell* by David Helwig opened, the last production Jim Garrard directed before he left for British Columbia. The play was based on the 1880 Donnelly murders, though it bore no relation to the various Donnelly plays which followed later at Passe Muraille and the Tarragon. Nathan Cohen gave the shabby production a negative review, noting that the rustic setting constructed of rough timber was apparently looted from the

Rochdale College seventeenth-floor terrace. A third new production, an actors' collective work about the *Futz* episode, to be titled *The Metropolitan Police Dossier,* was never staged. Garrard was both depressed and exhausted by this time, and ready to move on.

In the spring of 1970, Martin Kinch was hired as an assistant director at the Stratford Festival, where his wife, Miro, would be working in production. Kinch turned the operation of Passe Muraille over to Paul Thompson, who had functioned as stage manager and technical director after the remount of *Tom Paine.* Thompson assumed he would act as a caretaker while Kinch was away, but the failures that had occurred over the spring had persuaded Kinch that Passe Muraille might not survive the summer. In May 1970, director Ken Gass opened a new theatre, the Factory Theatre Lab. Gass had a declared policy of producing only Canadian plays, a direction both John Palmer and Paul Thompson had been advocating at Passe Muraille. The Factory attracted several Passe Muraille regulars, Edna Widenmaier for one, who felt unhappy with their current management.

TPM poster, 1971, drawn by Ralph McDermid.

Vampyr by Shain Jaffe, Martin Kinch and Phil Schreibman.

Directed by Martin Kinch.

CHAPTER FOUR

Passe Muraille at Trinity Square, Part Two

During the winter of 1970, the New Directors Group developed at Rochdale College, where both Jim Garrard and Martin Kinch were now living. The NDG allowed members to share their ideas about creativity and business in theatre, but members had to be invited to join. Garrard and Kinch were joined by Ken Gass and John Palmer, then by Martin Brenzell and Henry Tarvainen, both University of Toronto graduates. Earlier, Brenzell had directed at New York's Café La Mama and was now running the McMaster University theatre program. Rochdale resident Tarvainen trained with director Leon Major at Hart House, then became Major's assistant at the new St Lawrence Centre. Later, when he became known as a director, Paul Thompson was asked to join NDG. This group of strong creative egos managed to get along and support each other in their various projects. As Tarvainen remarked just after the group was formed; '... the spirit of the New Directors Group is an unlimited faith in each other's work and integrity. And if one person wants to do a play they will get the support and encouragement and financial aid and co-operation they need.'

It was Tarvainen who first suggested a Festival of Underground Theatre to the other NDG members. The first season on the St Lawrence Centre's main stage was not a success and community events at the Town Hall second stage had also done badly; Tarvainen felt he could sell the Centre on the Festival. The Ontario Arts Council financed a report on the project, to be written by Ken Gass, while Jim Garrard tried to raise other financing from the City of Toronto and the Canada Council, who were not very positive. Ken Gass's report led to an OAC grant of $15,000, the Festival's core funding.

The Festival of Underground Theatre, affectionately known as FUT, was scheduled to run from August 19 to September 6, 1970. Ron Terrill, former general manager of Passe Muraille, now assistant to Bruce Lawson, the Town Hall program director, was named as FUT's administrator, and Ken Gass was in charge of programming, with input from the other NDG partners.

Each NDG member had the opportunity to bring a production to the Festival stage. Paul Thompson brought Passe Muraille's *Ubu Raw*, an adaptation of the Alfred Jarry play, featuring Don Steinhouse as the king and a ten-foot-tall green phallus on wheels. Martin Kinch staged *Separate Cell*, a collective work based on the works of Scottish psychologist R.D. Laing. Factory Theatre Lab presented four new plays, three of them directed by Ken Gass. John Palmer brought his Ottawa production of Ibsen's *A Doll's House*, injecting a typical bourgeois archetype into the counterculture Festival. *Dead Sun Rise* by Louis Capson was staged by his Creation 2 company; Jean-Claude Germain's Theatre du Même Non from Montreal presented his play *Si Aurore m'était contée deux fois*; and John Juliani's Savage God company from Vancouver presented a work in progress. From New York City, FUT invited Peter Schumann's Bread and Puppet Theatre, and, on opening day, the company's giant puppets paraded south from Queen's Park to the St Lawrence Centre. The following evening they performed *The Difficult Life of Uncle Fatso*, an anti-American satire. Two weeks later, FUT closed with *The Colonial Fairy Tale*, a wild Tarzan spoof staged by Jérôme Savary's le Grand Théâtre Panique, or Panic Circus, from Paris.

Ubu Raw. Directed by Paul Thompson, 1971.
Festival of Underground Theatre. With Don Steinhouse, Bob Dermer,
Dini Baker and Ashleigh Moorhouse.
Photo by Lionel Douglas, courtesy of R. Nasmith Archives.

Other visitors included two more companies from New York City, Burning City Women, a feminist company, and the transvestite company Revolting Theatre, as well as the Buffalo comedy group Swamp Fox. Martin Brenzell planned to bring a program of off-off-Broadway plays from McMaster, but was forced to cancel at the last minute. FUT *Extravaganza*, a wild, improvised, counterculture variety show, filled Brenzell's spot on the main stage, hosted by Ron Terrill, with acts from Panic Circus, serious actors performing comedy numbers, and the audience running egg races at intermission. FUT closed with an idyllic Sunday afternoon picnic on the Toronto Islands.

For the New Directors Group, the Festival was a complete success; a broad selection of experimental groups were hosted at Toronto's new civic theatre, including major world artists like Savary and Schumann, who interacted easily with the community of visiting and local artists. Audience numbers were reasonable, and their interest was sustained over the two-week Festival. Critics weren't invited, as most shows only played twice, but press coverage was generous, especially in the *Toronto Star*. Critic Nathan Cohen decried the 'painful superiority of those visiting performers to the domestic breed, most of all the host groups from Toronto.' Like the production of *Futz* the year before, the 1970 Festival developed a bond between the artists who enabled its success and empowered the new Toronto theatre community.

There was talk of making FUT an annual event, but the St Lawrence Centre had incurred a deficit of nearly $15,000 on the Festival, and was not interested in repeating the experience. The New Directors Group was no longer a cohesive unit, its members embarking on very separate career paths. FUT brought an end to Passe Muraille's focus on the radical American theatre: from this point on the company leaders, Martin Kinch, John Palmer and others, would take productions in a Canadian nationalist direction, concentrating on plays by Canadian writers. Jim Garrard had already moved to the West Coast, leaving his theatre in the hands of Kinch, Palmer and Paul Thompson. The natural rivalry between Palmer and Kinch for both critical and audience attention left Thompson in charge of administration, stage management and technical direction at Trinity Square.

Paul Thompson was born in 1940 on Prince Edward Island and raised in western Ontario farm country, where his father was a veterinarian. At the University of Western Ontario he studied French, wrestled on the intercollegiate team and played in college musicals. Graduating in 1963, he won a French government scholarship to the Sorbonne, where he saw as many plays as he could to practise his French. He was impressed by French theatre's ability to 'explore ideas, or to defend this cause, or to get you to think in a certain way or react in a certain way.' In 1964, the famous anti-capitalist director Roger Planchon brought his theatre company from Lyon to Paris. Fascinated,

Thompson applied to join Planchon as an unpaid apprentice director. Obtaining 'the fastest MA in history' from the University of Toronto, Thompson joined Planchon in 1965, playing small parts and teaching private English lessons to survive.

He spent the summer with Keith Turnbull's theatre in London, Ontario, where, in 1966, he directed a medieval French play, *The Farce of Poor John*, staged on an historic pageant wagon; co-directed another play with Martin Kinch; and was technical director for the entire season. To support his second season in Lyon, Thompson obtained a Canada Council grant, allowing him to see theatre in Germany, Czechoslovakia and Italy. At the 1967 Avignon Festival, he appeared in Planchon's production of *Tartuffe*, and was offered possible acting and teaching positions in France. But he decided to go home ('If you're going to do something, you have to do it where you come from'), eager to use the techniques and attitudes he'd learned in Europe to help develop a new Canadian theatre.

In autumn of 1967, Thompson was hired to direct a Sault Ste. Marie community theatre, but he was unable to interest his amateur actors in plays with working-class stories and heroes. Because of his experience with Planchon, he was hired by the 1968 Stratford Festival to assist director Jean Gascon with *Tartuffe*, and was energized by the new writers and committed actors in the Festival workshop. There, he directed adaptations of Michael Ondaatje's *The Man with Seven Toes*, and Molière's *Don Juan*, and also met his future wife, actress Anne Anglin. Thompson spent the winter of 1968–69 at Montreal's Instant Theatre, founded in 1965 as a lunchtime theatre in the underground concourse of Place Ville Marie. There, he directed Beckett's *Endgame*, Elaine May's *Not Enough Rope*, Paul Foster's *The Recluse*, and co-created a mixed-media play with a Czech actress who had recently escaped the invasion of her country.

At the 1969 Stratford Festival, Thompson helped to remount *Tartuffe*, but he realized that this was not where he wanted to be; he felt he was being prevented from creating theatre about his own and his audience's world. He and Anne became avid supporters of the Canadian Place Theatre, the Stratford storefront run by Kinch and Palmer.

In the fall of 1969, Kinch invited Thompson to visit Passe Muraille on his way back to Montreal, to see Palmer's remount of *Memories for My Brother, Part 1* and the Kinch/Garrard version of *Tom Paine*. Kinch was replacing Garrard as artistic director and wanted Thompson to join him as technical director. Recognizing the possibilities of the company and its Trinity Square location, Thompson agreed, starting as stage manager of Kinch's *Richard III* and the *Sweet Eros* double bill. With Kinch working with other companies and Garrard distracted, Thompson was directing more plays than any other director at Passe Muraille: an improvised lunchtime show, *Charlie in So Many Ways* in March 1970, the unsuccessful *Notes from Quebec* in May, and *Ubu Raw* at FUT in August. Shain Jaffe had taught him enough accounting to manage the company finances and, when Martin Kinch left for Stratford, Thompson took over the theatre, with the title of Managing Director.

On October 8, 1970, Martin Kinch opened Frank Wedekind's adolescent sexual drama, *Spring Awakening*, an exception to the 'Canadian plays only' rule. The *Star*'s Nathan Cohen reviewed it as 'a sturdy interpretation, rich in substance and insight', but audiences were small during the three-week run. A late show of very short plays, written and directed by Louis Del Grande, under the name Louis Thompson, introduced a new Toronto star, the young local actress Brenda Donohue, opposite stage veteran Doris Petrie.

In November, Del Grande directed the satire on America *I Had It But It's All Gone Now*, by Richard De Canio, with Saul Rubinek and Bembo Davies. At Christmas, Clare Coulter and Anne Anglin produced a family puppet show and Thompson directed his own adaptation of Saint-Exupéry's *The Little Prince*. In January 1971, John Palmer opened *Out to Breakfast*, an experimental collective with his favourite

Anne Anglin in *Spring Awakening*. Directed by Martin Kinch, 1971.
Photo by Lionel Douglas, courtesy of R. Nasmith Archives.

actors, Anne Anglin, Louis Del Grande, Saul Rubinek and Bembo Davies, who all chose their own characters: Adolf Hitler, a Maoist milkman, a model and a preacher. The show was not well received by critics or audience, but some liked it, including Thompson, who kept it running.

It had been a year since Passe Muraille had produced a hit with *Sweet Eros*; now Kinch came up with another winner. *Vampyr* was created by Kinch, Shain Jaffe and musician Phil Schreibman. Inspired by the British Hammer horror studios, the actors improvised the script, in one session rehearsing for twenty-four hours straight. Booth Savage played the star vampire, combining sex with terror. *Vampyr* embodied the 1960s obsessions with the mysticism of romantic terrorism, soft-core pornography and the pursuit of pleasure that permeated the decaying Rochdale, where Kinch now lived. Schreibman's gothic music, Paul Williams's towering set and Kinch's elegantly obsessive production received rave reviews and sold-out houses during a six-week run.

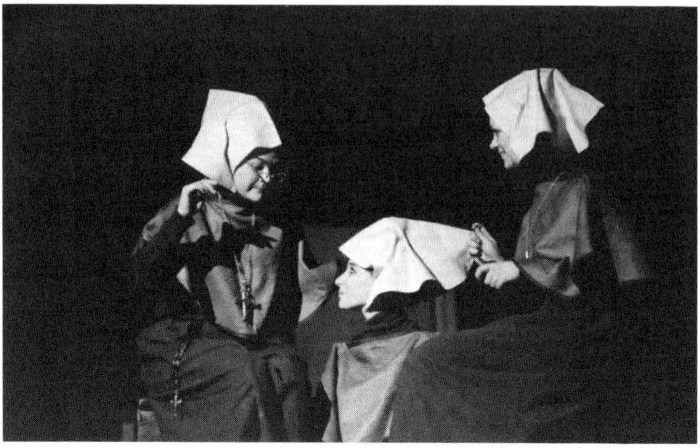

Vampyr. With Clare Coulter, Christine Pintner and Brenda Donohue.

Photo by Lionel Douglas, courtesy of R. Nasmith Archives.

Vampyr. With Booth Savage.

Photo by Lionel Douglas, courtesy of R. Nasmith Archives.

Thompson followed with *Doukhobors*, a collective work about an immigrant religious sect whose female members stripped to protest Canadian government persecution; as director Thompson called it, 'the first non-sexual nude show'. *Doukhobors* may have had more to do with 1960s hippies than immigrants looking for religious freedom, but it produced good reviews and five more weeks of audience line-ups, followed by a tour to Brock, Trent and Laurentian Universities.

On September 30, Thompson opened the collective *Free Ride*, about teenagers hitchhiking across Canada; with collaborator Larry Mollin, the director had spent the summer of 1970 hitchhiking as research. Then, on November 19, John Palmer opened his dangerously exciting production of the rock-and-roll musical *Charles Manson a.k.a. Jesus Christ* (book by Fabian Jennings; music by Canadian composer Allan Rae). The audience was seated on twenty-four-foot-tall scaffolding, and the actors leaped from a twenty-foot-high platform, and roller-skated around the hall as Manson's murderous gang. Peter Jobin starred as Manson, with Saul Rubinek as the *Rolling Stone* magazine reporter interviewing him and Sandy Crawley (son of film producer icons Judy and Budge Crawley) led the band. After the opening, leading actors were paid a percentage of the weekly box office receipts though actor Danny Freedman soon discovered that the young actors playing Manson's disciples weren't being paid at all. The actors who were being paid on a percentage asked Paul Thompson to reduce their percentages and share the proceeds with all the younger performers. Which Thompson did.

During the sold-out seven-week run of *Manson*, audience line-ups were a regular event, as they'd been with *Vampyr* and *Doukhobors*. This was the third popular hit from the Kinch/Palmer/Thompson creative team, each one bringing his own crowd-pleasing creation to the Trinity Square stage. For Thompson, the success of his actor-driven, collaborative work was confirmed by Passe Muraille's growing ability to reach audiences who weren't regular theatregoers, the people

Doukhobors. Directed by Paul Thompson. Lighting by Paul Williams. Actor Larry Mollin, centre. The set was made from the commandeered roof deck of Rochdale College. Photo by Robert Nasmith.

Doukhobors. Directed by Paul Thompson. Lighting by Paul Williams. With Dini Baker and Fina MacDonell. Photo by Robert Nasmith.

Free Ride. Directed by Paul Thompson, 1971.

Photo by Lionel Douglas, courtesy of R. Nasmith Archives.

Charles Manson a.k.a. Jesus Christ with Peter Jobin as Charles Manson.

Photo by Lionel Douglas.

he most wanted to attract. His collectives usually took ordinary Canadians as their central figures, and were often initially performed before the communities who reflected those figures.

In January 1972, Jim Garrard returned from Simon Fraser University with a new show, *The Black Queen Is Going to Eat You All Up*, developed during his West Coast theatre experiments. The 'writer' was Frank Powley, who had introduced Garrard to the 'rule play' improvisation technique, developed earlier by SFU teacher Paul Bettis. Garrard and Powley transformed this into the 'survival theatre' performance method, a more thoughtful improvisation process, in which the actor's objective was 'to survive in theatrical terms'. A few *Black Queen* performers came from British Columbia with Powley and Garrard and some had worked with Garrard on earlier Passe Muraille productions. Rehearsals were open to the public, and the actors clearly struggled with the freedom of 'survival theatre'. On opening night, actors from Frank Masi's Royal Canadian Mounted Theatre actually took over the stage from Garrard's cast. Reviews were bad; the *Toronto Star*'s Urjo Kareda panned 'a cast almost unparalleled for their ineptitude for improvisation'. Playgoers who wanted to see the show again could return for free, and many did so, agreeing with Garrard that he'd directed 'a fabulous, fascinating show'. For earlier Passe Muraille fans, the production was an important event, but it had no popular success, and Garrard returned to Vancouver, avoiding the theatre for the next few years.

In February, director Peter Boretski opened *Bethune*, his collective study of the heroic Canadian field surgeon who died caring for communist Chinese fighters battling the Japanese invaders. *Toronto Star* critic Kareda stated: 'Theatre manages to make Dr Norman Bethune a bore', and the play's three-week run did not do well. In April, Louis Del Grande directed *Tantrums*, four experimental short plays by Del Grande's new discovery, Hrant Alianak. Alianak was born in Egypt in 1950, immigrated to Canada in 1967 and began acting with amateur theatres in Toronto, where he was spotted by Del Grande. Kareda greeted *Tantrums* with a rave: 'Exciting new play at Passe Muraille almost too good', but the show never found a popular audience. Paul Thompson had high hopes that Alianak's comic B-movie-style dialogue and film noir visuals might produce the urban-style hits that Kinch and Palmer had taken with them when they left to found their new Toronto Free Theatre in early 1972. Alianak did develop many dedicated fans, but his popular appeal remained limited.

On May 19, Thompson opened the last play of the season, *Buffalo Jump*, developed collectively with actors and writer Carol Bolt. Her play, *Next Year Country*, about the 1935 'On to Ottawa Trek' by unemployed workers, had been produced by the Globe Theatre in Regina. A move to Toronto Workshop Productions was planned, but Bolt was unable to come to an agreement with George Luscombe over future script rights, and she approached Passe Muraille. As Thompson later recalled, '... we reinvented the play. We had the actors improvise scenes and Carol wrote from the improvisations, while I tried to key in on what the actors were bringing in and utilize that energy.' Thompson focused more on his actors' contributions than other directors of Passe Muraille collectives had, and Carol Bolt was the first playwright he involved in one of his collective productions. *Globe and Mail* critic Herbert Whittaker appreciated the 'visual distinction' supplied by artist John Boyle to 'An ingenious *Buffalo Jump*'. A resident of St. Catharines, Boyle had known Thompson during his summer theatre days in London, Ontario, and created pop-art images of people and objects important to the workers' march on Ottawa, which Thompson used as settings for his production. In Kareda's opinion: 'The dewy sentimentality of poverty and hardship in *Buffalo Jump* seems awfully easy and maybe even a little cheap.' For Thompson, *Buffalo Jump* marked a new development in his visual style, and, in the case of the play's composite trek leader, named Red Evans, a new focus on the central character as 'hero'.

The Farm Show. Directed by Paul Thompson, 1972. With Fina MacDonell, Anne Anglin, David Fox, Janet Amos and Miles Potter. Photo courtesy of R. Nasmith Archives.

In the spring of 1972, Thompson had an idea which would change Passe Muraille's story. He was commuting between the theatre and Brock University in St. Catharines, where he was organizing a festival of new plays and giving theatre classes. Theatre Ontario, a new arts organization, had invited British director Peter Cheeseman, a celebrated creator of factually based community documentary theatre, to hold workshops at both Passe Muraille and Brock University. Thompson talked to Brock lecturer Ted Johns about creating a collective piece about farming life in Ontario, where they'd both been raised. Johns's relatives in the nearby farming town of Clinton offered a vacant farmhouse and barn for the summer. Passe Muraille had no budget available, but Thompson decided to finance *The Farm Show* with his Brock University salary. The cast he assembled included his wife, Anne Anglin; Janet Amos (who had dropped out of *Doukhobors*);

Miles Potter, a recently arrived American, who'd produced children's theatre at Passe Muraille and appeared in *Buffalo Jump*; Alan Jones, who'd acted in *Doukhobors* and *Buffalo Jump*; and his girlfriend, actress Fina MacDonell, who'd met Thompson in Winnipeg when he was researching *Free Ride*. The final member of the company was a Brantford high school teacher from Northern Ontario, who'd acted in community theatre. After nine years, David Fox decided to give up teaching and contacted Passe Muraille, looking up Martin Kinch, an old friend from Western University.

Thompson remembered Fox as a very good student actor at Western and offered him a summer in Clinton as his first professional job.

Before his actors arrived, Thompson had already arranged with many of the local farmers to meet with his cast, and the actors were expected to pitch in with farm work during their visits. At day's end, cast members returned to the farmhouse and reported on their experiences to the company, rehearsals involved improvisations based on their varied stories. As Thompson later described the process, 'I don't think it's documentary theatre; I think it's folk theatre because in many cases we're not interested in fact. If an emotional, exciting lie makes better theatre and gets the point of the scene across better, then I'm more interested in the lie than the fact.' For Janet Amos, interviewing strangers was embarrassing, both for herself and the farm couples. Jones hated the farm labour and told Thompson he'd be leaving right after the opening, which he did. Furious after his first day of work, Potter eventually turned his misery into the show's hilarious haying scene. The process they were developing was new to many of the actors, difficult and frustrating for all, but Ray Bird, the farmer whose barn and house they were using, recalled that the powerful scenes they were creating seemed to worry the cast a little as their opening loomed. On Sunday afternoon, August 13, 1972, *The Farm Show* was performed in Ray Bird's barn, with no sets, no lights;

just stacked bails of hay as seating. A crowd of fifty was anticipated, at least two hundred arrived, and the shared performance demonstrated the easy bond that had grown up between these farmers and performers, who'd all been uncomfortable strangers just weeks before.

Four days later, a neighbouring town's newspaper, the *Goderich Signal-Star*, heralded the event:

> With songs, poems, skits, interpretive exercises, and monologues, the three actors and three actresses from Toronto bewitched their audience … those in the audience who were from the area recognized most of their neighbours in the scenes. Howls of laughter and groans of embarrassment burst continually from the straw bleachers … somehow the actors managed, while laying open the characters of the community for all to see, not to offend anybody (they hope) and not to bear false witness to the personalities of any of their new-found friends.

After three more weeks of rehearsal, *The Farm Show* opened at Trinity Square in Toronto to rave reviews, with Thompson replacing Alan Jones. As Urjo Kareda wrote, 'In *The Farm Show*, Thompson and his actors have helped us to know, understand and love a community of people beyond our sphere of familiarity. As artists, they can have no higher ambitions.' The production ran for a very successful four weeks; with a large and flexible playing space, Passe Muraille was in by far the best position of all the city's new theatres to exploit a hit when it came along. After two years of managing Passe Muraille with very tight financial control, Thompson realized that one or two major hits could support the theatre's operations for an entire year.

Beginning in 1971, the Canadian government created two new employment subsidies, the Local Initiatives Program (LIP) and Opportunities for Youth (OFY), which small Canadian theatres were encouraged to access. Thompson had doubts, worried that the two programs would upset the fragile economy now developing in the new small theatre scene, and that government dependency and bureaucracy could outweigh any financial advantages the grants might bring. Passe Muraille actors were paid a very small weekly salary, less than the Actors' Equity minimum, although Equity members did sign pro forma contracts. But each performer also received a percentage of a hit production's weekly box office. So actors enjoyed regular employment, with weekly bonuses for hit shows, and Thompson was committed to arranging accommodation for actors on tour. For Thompson, popular success confirmed his theatre's cultural legitimacy, especially for audiences unfamiliar with Passe Muraille or with theatre in general; as he told the original *Farm Show* cast, 'You'll get tired of it before the audience does.' The show was remounted for several tours, with various cast changes, ending with a tour of England in 1979. The production's ability to examine the identity of a community, transform it into entertainment and then reflect it back to that same community, became the dominant theme of Thompson's productions for the next few years, as he celebrated his Canadian identity and attempted to capture new audiences.

On October 25, Louis Del Grande opened *Dog in the Manger*, his own wild adaptation of Lope de Vega's cynical comedy about love gone wrong, starring his wife, Martha Gibson. With costumes and setting (an explosion of elegant 1930s style, French high fashion) by Del Grande, the production ran for five weeks. Another humorist opened the next show; England's Ken Campbell conceived and directed *Pilk's Madhouse*, a comic review which supposedly presented the writings of fictional expatriate Canadian playwright Henry Pilk (Campbell's own invention). Campbell was known in England for his touring comedy shows, and *Pilk's Madhouse* was invited to move to London's Royal Court Theatre in December. It was replaced by *The Separate*

1837: The Farmers' Revolt by Rick Salutin and the company. Directed by Paul Thompson. With Eric Peterson and Terry Tweed. Photo by Lionel Douglas, courtesy of R. Nasmith Archives.

Condition by Barbara Nye, directed by John Juliani of Vancouver's Savage God group. The work was a strange collection of character monologues with transsexual content, which received negative reviews and small audiences. This was not a play that Thompson would ever have staged himself, but he felt that diversity was essential for Passe Muraille's survival.

While these productions were playing at Trinity Square, Thompson was working on his next production, *1837*, a collaborative play about the popular rebellion in Toronto. He had decided against producing Herschel Hardin's play *William Lyon Mackenzie* when local writer Rich Salutin suggested the rebellion as subject matter for a new 'collective' production. With *Farm Show* actors David Fox, Janet Amos, Miles Potter and Passe Muraille newcomer Eric Peterson as Mackenzie, *1837* opened on January 18, 1973, for a highly successful five-week run. In 1974, a remount was staged, *1837: The Farmers' Revolt*, which focused on the rebellion's rural origins, and toured Southern Ontario. Peterson became a regular Passe Muraille actor and his heroic performance as Mackenzie exemplified Thompson's competing themes of collective and personal heroism. On March 2, Jim Garrard, recently returned to Toronto, opened *The Master* by Philip Hopcraft. Garrard had given up the theatre, but was unable to convince Hopcraft that another director would serve his play better. When he saw the production before it opened, Hopcraft withdrew his name from the program and gave up writing plays. Miles Potter's Children's Pantomime Theatre mounted daytime performances of original plays *The Moon Princess* and *The Musicians of Bremen*, Potter's fourth Passe Muraille children's production since he'd arrived the year before.

On March 22, Thompson opened *Pauline*, a new collective biography of Six Nations–born lecturer and poet Pauline Johnson. Carol Bolt returned as playwright, Anne Anglin played Pauline and all the other roles were taken by Janet Amos and Peter Kundar, co-founder of the Factory Theatre Lab. Reviews were not favourable, the *Star*'s Kareda

Pauline by Carol Bolt with the company. Directed by Paul Thompson.
With Peter Kundar, Janet Amos and Anne Anglin.
Photo by Lionel Douglas, courtesy of R. Nasmith Archives.

felt that 'Passe Muraille's biographical play remains oblique', and *Pauline* ran for just three weeks.

On April 11, *The Farm Show* re-opened for a victorious two-week run, before beginning a very important Southern Ontario tour. By the end of 1973, the theatre at 11 Trinity Square was scheduled to be demolished to allow construction of the new Eaton Centre shopping mall. Establishing a touring circuit outside Toronto, which could supply large audiences and community-based artistic credibility on a consistent basis, might be Passe Muraille's only key to survival. For Thompson, this was also a political act: 'This tour is about how culture has been grabbed off by the city people with leisure.' *The Farm Show* toured to smaller locations — Wingham, Listowel, Orangeville and many others that were often missed by theatre tours — performing in small-town Victorian opera houses, meeting halls, high school gyms and auction barns.

The tour closed on the Stratford Festival Theatre stage, where

Cod on a Stick, CODCO, 1973. With Tommy Sexton, Mary Walsh, Cathy Jones and Andy Jones. Photo courtesy of R. Nasmith Archives.

Them Donnellys, 1973. Directed by Paul Thompson. With (L-R) Booth Savage and David Fox. Photo courtesy of R. Nasmith Archives.

Thompson announced, 'We're sponsored by a local drama group — the Stratford Festival.' In August 1973, *The Farm Show* played at Ottawa's National Arts Centre; in the spring of 1974, the company toured Saskatchewan. *The Clinton Special*, a documentary film about *The Farm Show*'s creation, produced by Michael Ondaatje, was first televised in 1974, spreading the show's legend, followed by the publication of the play in 1976.

During the summer of 1973, between *The Farm Show* tours, Thompson and his performers spent two months in Cobalt, once a major mining centre in Northern Ontario, working on a collective show called *Under the Greywacke*. To the company, the greywacke, a layer of clustered rock which covers silver ore, was an image of the longed-for new silver strike that would save Cobalt from its forty-year decline. With personality portraits, songs, skits and dramatic recreations, all based on their own observations, the company created a portrait of Cobalt and its people, and attempted to join the community with some success. Actress Jacquie Presley took second prize in the Miss Cobalt Contest. '*Under the Greywacke* is about drinking, tall stories and the gambling instinct,' as Thompson described it. 'Cobalt ... is a ghost town that refuses to die.' The local population enjoyed the show, performed in a vacant movie theatre, but *Greywacke* reached little popular audience beyond Cobalt. In September 1973, it opened a three-week Toronto run at the Church of the Holy Trinity and received positive reviews, but Thompson never revived the show and it never toured. On October 10, Hrant Alianak directed his own first full-length play, *Noah's Kiosk*, a take-off of movies about the American South after the Civil War, receiving weak reviews and small audiences. In the small, second-floor performance space, Louis Del Grande opened *So Who's Goldberg* for late-night audiences. The sensitive one-act play about a homosexual pianist and the man he picks up — which had already been given a workshop production at the Lincoln Center in New York — received excellent reviews at Passe Muraille.

October also saw the Toronto debut of the company of performers from Newfoundland who would later call themselves CODCO, in their revue *Crime and Punishment*. Thompson had originally met the CODCO actors when they auditioned for *The Farm Show* and helped to finance their development. A new collective, *Them Donnellys*, was being rehearsed outside Toronto with writer Frank McEnaney, and was intended to attract the small-town audiences of Southern Ontario. The production opened in November 1973, at the Victoria Playhouse in Petrolia. It followed the same tour route as *The Farm Show*, ending with three performances at the Stratford Festival Theatre.

In Toronto, facing the demolition of 11 Trinity Square, Thompson rented office and rehearsal space near Toronto Workshop Productions and opened Theatre Passe Muraille East in a church hall at Dundas and Sherbourne Streets. In November, the first production there was a theatre convention and a festival of two-minute plays organized by Frank Powley, writer of the *Black Queen* with Jim Garrard, for his organization GNATCAN, the Grand National Academy of Theatre of Canada. At Trinity Square on November 26, Louis Del Grande opened *All the Ghosts* by Larry Fineberg, about a retired psychiatrist and a young couple she takes in as summer boarders. The doctor was played by Jane Mallet, one of Toronto's most admired veteran actors; Mallet was one of the first of Toronto's established actors to work in the city's new theatres, and she was soon joined by others. On January 9, 1974, the last production at Trinity Square opened, *Toronto Pixie Caper*, a madcap 'theatre fair' staged by Ken Campbell. Phil Schreibman played the piano and sang, Booth Savage told the company's oral history and Anne Anglin drew 'psychic portraits'. On January 14, Urjo Kareda wrote: 'Passe Muraille ... has given us a wealth of exciting, revelatory, transforming theatre.... I can remember so clearly how exciting my first Theatre Passe Muraille production was, and I know how happily I'll remember this lovely place.'

The West Show. Directed by Paul Thompson.
Paul Thompson (on horse) and Eric Peterson.
Photo courtesy of R. Nasmith Archives.

The West Show. Directed by Paul Thompson. With Paul Thompson,
Anne Anglin and Eric Peterson.
Photo courtesy of R. Nasmith Archives.

CHAPTER FIVE

Theatre Passe Muraille on the Road

On February 14, 1974, Paul Thompson opened *Adventures of an Immigrant*, Passe Muraille's first production after losing their Trinity Square theatre. With writer Rick Salutin, Thompson used his collective improvisation process to examine Toronto's various and ever-expanding ethnic communities, hoping to appeal to a wider audience base. In a February *Toronto Star* interview he stated, 'Theatre Passe Muraille has literally become a theatre without walls.... But instead of being a calamity, maybe it's a godsend in disguise to help bring theatre to Joe Lunch Pail.' He was unable to recruit any ethnic performers, however, and the *Immigrant* cast included Passe Muraille collective regulars Anne Anglin, Janet Amos, Eric Peterson and David Fox. They interviewed members of the Italian community, among others, and took part in various local community affairs; Anglin took a job in a local garment factory and wrote a song about her experience for the show. The production opened at an Italian neighbourhood club, then moved on to various other ethnic community venues; one performance took place on a Toronto Transit Commission PCC streetcar, chartered by the theatre. *Toronto Star* critic Urjo Kareda, an immigrant himself, found the show a disappointment: 'Last night's performance, gentle and mild as it was, nevertheless fell rather flat because of a missing ingredient — the Italian immigrants themselves.... Without them, the performers seemed — probably without meaning to — slightly patronizing.' Italian and other European immigrant populations apparently resented both the examination and the representation of their communities by outsiders and stayed away.

Much more successful were two revivals of CODCO's *Cod on a Stick* comedy show. While he was casting *Them Donnellys*, in the autumn of 1973, Paul Thompson auditioned a group of actors from Newfoundland, 'but I couldn't use them. Their accents just weren't Southern Ontario.' Impressed by their unusual sense of humour and ability to interact with each other, he appropriated $300 from another budget and gave them funding to 'Create your own show that's a send-up of Main-landers' attitudes to your native culture.' Their hit *Cod on a Stick* revue opened at Passe Muraille East in November 1973, and was revived for another three-week run in January 1974, then embarked on a tour of Newfoundland sponsored by the CBC. CODCO brought other new revues to Passe Muraille over the next few years; *Sickness, Death and Beyond the Grave* in October 1974; *Would You Like to Smell My Pocket Crumbs* in 1976; and *Laugh Your Guts Out with Total Strangers* in 1976. The popular CODCO performers brought a unique new brand of popular comedy to the Toronto stage.

Passe Muraille enlarged its touring operations into western Canada in the spring of 1974, sending *The Farm Show* out to Saskatchewan. In Saskatoon, Thompson met with actors at the 25th Street Theatre, leading to a series of collective productions based on western subjects: Passe Muraille's *The West Show* in 1975 and *Far as the Eye Can See* in 1977, and 25th Street Theatre's *If You're So Good Why Are You In Saskatoon?* in 1975 and *Paper Wheat* in 1977.

Paul Thompson's first improvised show with a single actor was *Naked on the North Shore* with Ted Johns in 1977. After two successful runs at Passe Muraille East that spring, *North Shore* was revived for several extended tours.

At the same time, in the small town of Blyth, Ontario, Thompson, Rick Salutin and a few actors were rehearsing a new version of

1837: The Farmers' Revolt. During the summer, Thompson was also commissioned to produce *Oil*, a collective work about the town of Petrolia, the location of Ontario's successful nineteenth-century oil-drilling industry. *Globe and Mail* critic Herbert Whittaker covered the opening at Petrolia's vintage Victoria Playhouse: 'Oil is a play for them, about them and there is a town full of neighbours to share it with. So when the first night audience rose to its feet it was only partially a tribute to the Passe Muraille actors; it was very much a tribute to the townspeople's ancestors and friends.' Despite *Oil*'s hometown success, Thompson was disappointed that, like *Under the Greywacke* the year before, his production never played anywhere else after its initial local run. However, *1837: The Farmers' Revolt* did follow *Oil* at the Victoria Playhouse before going out on tour.

Thompson announced a new 'Seed Show' program in the fall of 1974, giving a formal structure to Passe Muraille's development of new theatre talents and productions with twelve $1,000 grants for the 1974–75 season. In Thompson's own words:

> ... you can't justify it in terms of audience, because some of the projects will be popular and some of them won't—and it won't necessarily be the popular ones that will be the most important. It's just absolutely necessary for us to continue discovering forms and giving people with ideas a chance to explore and display their ideas. Theatre Passe Muraille has always been a place that welcomes new ideas and really survives on the continuation of new ideas.

The 'Seed Show' project produced several successful new shows. With actors Miles Potter, Clare Coulter and Geza Kovacs as co-creators, Janet Amos directed the successful revue *Alligator Pie*, based on a collection of poems for children by Dennis Lee. Passe Muraille revived this family hit as a Christmas show for several seasons; it also played successfully in other Canadian cities. *Almighty Voice*, a collective work about a twenty-two-year-old Cree rebel hero who was slain

Oil. Directed by Paul Thompson. Petrolia Opera House, 1974. From bottom left: Paul Thompson, Booth Savage, Jimmy Butler (fiddler), Terry Tweed, Howie Cooper, Janet Amos, Ted Johns, Diane English, Miles Potter, Diane D'Aquila, Eric Peterson, Paul Williams, Anne Anglin, Bob Pearson. Photo courtesy of R. Nasmith Archives.

in a Saskatchewan Northwest Mounted Police shootout in 1897, was directed by a young Clarke Rogers, who had resigned as the artistic director of Theatre Calgary in 1972 after a major public disagreement with that theatre's board. Rogers toured his production of *Almighty Voice* through the prairies, expanding Passe Muraille's increasingly important western connections.

A less successful 'Seed Show' was *Follies of Conviction*, the fictional history of a civic campaign to close down a Toronto burlesque show in 1912, written and directed by James Roy. The next summer, following Paul Thompson's advice, Roy founded the Blyth Festival, a permanent theatre company which regularly exchanged productions with Passe Muraille. Thompson produced his own 'Seed Show' collective, *Canadian Heroes Series 1: Gabriel Dumont*, which ran for just four performances, but involved actors Eric Peterson, Ted Johns and David Fox, painter John Boyle, designer Brian Arnott and co-director John Gray. Except for *The Spell of the Yukon*, adapted from Robert Service's poems, which opened on September 11 for a six-week run at the Poor Alex Theatre, Passe Muraille's full-size productions in late 1974 were mostly revivals of past hits. *1837: The Farmers' Revolt* opened at the historic 1830s Enoch Turner Schoolhouse on September 12, and *Them Donnellys* arrived at the Church of the Holy Trinity on October 16. Both touring companies were very well received by Toronto critics and audiences. On October 24, the CODCO company, already a favourite with Toronto audiences, opened another hit, *Sickness, Death and Beyond the Grave*, at the Bathurst Street Theatre.

In 1972, CITY-TV, a new, independent Toronto television station, began to broadcast soft-core pornographic movies at midnight on Fridays. Just six months later, these 'Baby Blue Movies' were reaching an audience of 280,000 each week, sixty percent of the Toronto region's late-Friday-night television viewers. The broad audience that CITY-TV managed to attract gave Paul Thompson an idea for a Passe Muraille collective about Toronto. 'We took the techniques of *The*

Farm Show and tried to apply them to the sexual fascination of the big city.' But the usual Passe Muraille regulars were not ready to work on a project where they'd have to take their clothes off; the days of *Doukhobors* were long gone. According to Thompson, '... it was a hard show for everybody to do. Taking your clothes off in public is hard. Before I started, I approached some of the regular actors at the theatre but they didn't feel comfortable with the idea — however much they were prepared to put themselves on the line in other ways for other plays.' A group of actors with no experience in Thompson's collective collaborative process went out to research the world of sex in Toronto, returning to improvise and rehearse at Passe Muraille's Breadalbane Street studio, for a longer period than usual, given the actors' inexperience with Thompson's techniques.

I Love You, Baby Blue opened on January 18, 1975, at the Bathurst Street United Church. Critic Urjo Kareda felt 'there is less tenderness here than in any Paul Thompson show I've ever seen, and for that reason alone, this is the most depressing.' It was neither a grungy Yonge

I Love You, Baby Blue. Directed by Paul Thompson, 1975. With Joanne MacIntyre. Photo courtesy of R. Nasmith Archives.

I Love You, Baby Blue. Directed by Paul Thompson, 1975. With Terry Schonblum. Photo courtesy of R. Nasmith Archives.

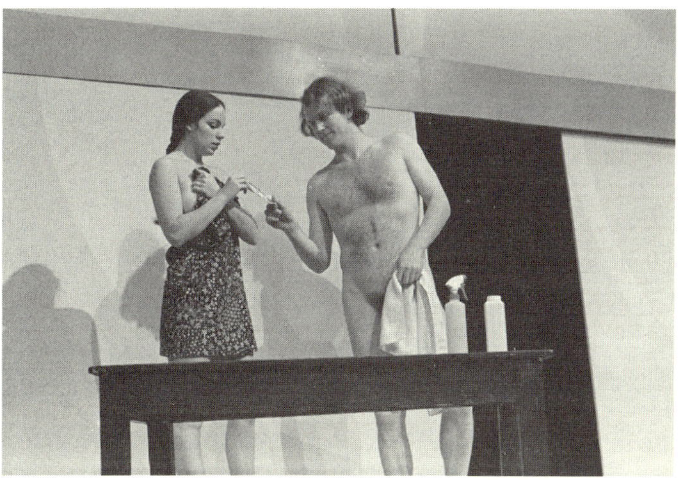

I Love You, Baby Blue. Directed by Paul Thompson, 1975. With Terry Schonblum, Andy Thompson. Photo courtesy of R. Nasmith Archives.

Street strip show nor a salacious sex burlesque like *Oh! Calcutta!*, but a comic study of Toronto's diverse sexual world, from strip clubs to massage parlours to singles bars to couples watching TV at home. There were naked bodies and vulgar words. The United Church congregation worried about the sexual content in their sacred hall, and the Toronto Police were keeping an eye on the show. *Baby Blue* sold out most of its more than three-month run, audiences lined up for seats, the actors, working, as usual, for a percentage of the box office, made good money every week and theatre profits kept increasing, but the show's success led to criticism that Thompson and his theatre were exploiting sex for profit. Actress Terry Schonblum commented, 'The show was very raw, and titillating and sexy, and sometimes that's hard to admit. Lots of people came for tits and ass. It was truly the best show in town for that.'

For Thompson, the show's success meant that he'd succeeded in making a connection with Toronto's collective identity: 'It was really hard to tell people — although I think that it's true — that the money was a side effect. It just happens that there is money to be made with any show that fascinates the public to the extent that *Baby Blue* did.'

Passe Muraille hadn't been visited by the Toronto Police morality squad since the *Futz* arrests in March 1969, although the same morality squad had forced the Toronto Free Theatre to close down their production of *Clear Light* in November 1973. Soon after *Baby Blue* opened in January, morality-squad officers visited Passe Muraille and demanded to see a script of the play. As the production was an improvised, collective work, this was impossible, but the officers had a polite meeting with Thompson and company members and detailed the scenes in which they felt the dialogue was not acceptable. Members of the cast were against accepting any censorship of material which they had created, but, in Thompson's opinion, 'we were getting to say what we wanted ... it was silly to argue over three or four "fucks".' The changes requested were made to the show, the officers left, and nothing further was heard from them during the three-month run of the play. At the end of April, as the planned fifteen-week run of *Baby Blue* was about to close, the morality squad returned. Circumstances had changed; the Conservative government of the Province of Ontario had called an election. Thompson later recalled, '... a provincial election was called and one of the campaign promises called for a clean-up of Yonge Street and an end to the kind of free sexuality that had been allowed to start in Toronto. We were arrested on a Friday night, two days before we were due to close anyway, and the (Conservative Premier) Bill Davis's stand against explicit promiscuity hit the papers on Saturday. So it seems very likely that it was politically motivated. All the actors, the stage manager, and myself as director and producer were charged with "performing an immoral stage performance".'

Passe Muraille had been ready to close the show, but now they realized that they had to keep it running, just on principle. On Saturday, the night following the arrests, the regular performance was replaced by a public meeting on the stage. With input from the audience, a decision was reached to schedule three special final performances for the next weekend. Numbers of Passe Muraille backers requested the opportunity to participate in the final performances, demanding to sign theatre contracts so they could also be arrested. Thompson added all of them to a large crowd scene, and Toronto city aldermen, arts officials, religious ministers, actors and other theatre artists cheerfully crowded onto the stage. The morality squad never turned up, but crowds of Toronto media did, the final performances sold out and Theatre Passe Muraille's most successful production came to a rousing theatrical close. Thompson had made the Toronto connection he was hoping for.

The *Baby Blue* trial, in November 1975, and was both short and anticlimactic. As Thompson described it: 'The prosecution played a tape of the show and had a policewoman attest to what she saw and what she thought it meant. We were heavily backed by the city and the establishment and after half a day the prosecution could see that their approach wasn't working—that their case was weak—and they withdrew it.'

Six years had passed since the *Futz* trial, Passe Muraille was no longer a radical agent of social change; it was becoming a Toronto cultural institution. The *Futz* production had taken the theatre into what was then forbidden territory; *Baby Blue* was simply a reflection of how Toronto society was changing. Thompson felt that:

> we weren't doing anything on stage that hadn't been done before or saying words that hadn't been said before. But unlike the limited runs of what were, in some cases, more extreme productions by other underground theatres, we were playing it to six hundred people at every performance with no let-up in sight. That soon adds up to a significant number of people, significant in the sense that it was becoming part of the public domain. What is permitted within a closed or cloistered situation (i.e., if you don't bother us, we won't bother you) is not permitted, it seems, if a lot of people get to hear about it.

None of Passe Muraille's other productions during 1975 were as successful as *Baby Blue*, but the year was a busy one. *Tony's Woman* and *Follies of Conviction* in February, *Family Entertainment* in March, and *Monomania* in May, were all 'Seed Shows'; Rick Salutin's play *The False Messiah* opened on March 13, the collective *Alive* on April 23, Hrant Alianak's *Night* on May 7, the collective *City: The Toronto Show* on September 18, and Hrant Alianak's adaptation of Shakespeare's *Titus Andronicus* as a Sergio Leone western on October 29. The *Futz* bust had led to Theatre Passe Muraille finding a new home at Trinity Square. The successful run of *Baby Blue* had similar results. When the show's actors felt self-conscious about the inflated weekly salaries that their percentages of the box-office revenues were paying them, Thompson suggested they take smaller percentages and contribute to the

A new home at 16 Ryerson Avenue.
Photo courtesy of R. Nasmith Archives.

theatre's new 'building fund'. By the time the show closed, the fund had grown to $30,000, enough to serve as a down payment on a building that could be the theatre's new home.

Thompson's friend Toronto artist Charles Pachter, who'd made a number of real estate investments in the up-and-coming Queen Street West arts area, spotted an abandoned warehouse on Ryerson Avenue, just east of Queen and Bathurst Streets, which he felt would be an ideal location for Passe Muraille. The owner of the building planned to demolish it and re-develop the lot, but Pachter managed to save the warehouse by getting it designated as an historic building by the city of Toronto. Late in 1975, Passe Muraille bought its new home for $100,000. Within ten years the theatre building was worth at least one million dollars. This growing equity allowed the theatre to budget their operations at a deficit level which would be impossible for most small theatres.

The building on Ryerson was converted to a facility with two theatres, one large, the other smaller, and rehearsal studios, dressing rooms and offices. As well as affording operating space for Theatre

Horsburg Scandal. Directed by Paul Thompson, 1976. With Don Harron, Michael Fahey, Abigail Wright and Eric Peterson.
Photo courtesy of R. Nasmith Archives.

Passe Muraille, it supplied inexpensive performance spaces for newcomers to the Toronto theatre scene: companies such the Hummer Sisters, Michael Hollingsworth's Videocabaret, the Clichettes, Buddies in Bad Times, Necessary Angel, and Triple Action Theatre; and directors like Des McAnuff, who staged his own rock-musical adaptation of Christopher Marlowe's *Faustus*. Over the years, important new plays debuted there, many created by Passe Muraille 'family' members: Jim Garrard's *Cold Comfort*, Hrant Alianak's *The Blues*, John Gray's *18 Wheels* and Linda Griffith's *Maggie and Pierre*. Relationships continued with Saskatoon's 25th Street Theatre, the Blyth Festival and CODCO; new plays were developed in Alberta and the Northwest Territories; Passe Muraille productions toured Canada. Paul Thompson worked mainly in the collective improvisational form he continued to develop. In 1976, he produced *The Horsburg*

Scandal and *The Olympics Show*; in 1977, the Stratford Festival comedy, *Shakespeare for Fun and Profit* and *Les Maudits Anglais*, with English-speaking actors performing in French for audiences in the Province of Quebec. While rehearsing in French, Linda Griffiths happened on the inspiration for her one-woman show, *Maggie and Pierre*: 'I began fooling around with a Pierre Trudeau character and one day Thompson said, "That's it. That's your one-person show. You play both of them." I thought he was out of his mind. A year later, we began rehearsal.' After 'jam session' rehearsals, Griffiths and Thompson opened at the smaller house on Ryerson Avenue, moved on to Toronto's Royal Alexandra Theatre, then travelled to New York City, and made a series of successful tours.

This hit show allowed Thompson to make his connection with the consciousness of the national Canadian audience more effectively than he had since the success of *The Farm Show*. Next to Toronto Workshop Productions, Passe Muraille was now the longest-running Toronto theatre. Its radical beginnings, under the direction of Jim Garrard, Martin Kinch and John Palmer, were succeeded by Paul Thompson's successful nationalism, producing new Canadian works, original scripts, adaptations or collectives, reflecting themes and cultures from different regions across the country, and then bringing those images back to Toronto.

Oil at Petrolia Opera House, 1974.

Directed by Paul Thompson. With Booth Savage, Miles Potter, Howie Cooper and Bob Pearson. Photo courtesy of R. Nasmith Archives.

AFTERWORD

In 1967, after my second season at Ontario's Stratford Shakespeare Festival, I was informed I was not going to be asked back for the next year. I had just received $20,000 as compensation for a motorcycle accident I'd had back in 1964, so I packed up and headed for London, in my mind the centre of the theatre world. In my first week there, I attended one of the first open casting calls that British Equity had ever held and was offered a small role in producer Peter Bridge's professional production of *Zigger-Zagger*. The Peter Terson comedy-drama about football hooliganism had originally been presented at London's National Youth Theatre.

The Equity production I was in had a cast of eighty young actors and opened at the Strand Theatre (now the Novello) in the West End in March 1968. Unfortunately, it closed just two weeks later. The *Zigger-Zagger* title sounded like a middle-class British comedy, which was usual programming for the Strand Theatre. When the curtain went up, the older audiences who were expecting a Michael Denison or Dulcie Gray comedy were confronted by eighty kids on football stands, glaring down at them and bellowing, 'We all live at the back of city end!' You could see the audience instantly recoil, and most left as soon as they could. It was only five weeks' work, but it was a great introduction to the London scene and gave me a dozen friends who became firm pals.

I didn't have much luck getting an agent or another job. I did pick up work as an extra at Covent Garden, both in operas and ballets. It was a lot of fun and I got to listen to some wonderful singers. I spent a very enjoyable year in London, going to the theatre and all the latest films, as well as many classics at the National Film Theatre. Then an old friend came to London, William Hutt, a regular star at the Stratford Festival. One of the hit plays in London then was *Hadrian VII*, adapted from an early novel about a cigarette-smoking pope. Bill Hutt saw *Hadrian* and felt I was right for the juvenile lead. He subsequently asked producer Bill Freedman to consider me for it.

I met Bill Freedman, fellow producer Charlie Kasher and director Peter Dews at the Mermaid Theatre and read for them. They told me they'd have to hold open readings in New York; they'd call me when they got back. On the way out, I ran into another old Stratford friend, Douglas Rain, who had just replaced *Hadrian* star Alec McCowen. Dougie thanked me for sending him a congratulatory postcard after I saw his amazing performance as the robot HAL in the film *2001: A Space Odyssey*. As I left the theatre, the stage manager told me Bill, Charlie and Peter wanted to see me again. When I walked in, they all said, 'We're not going to find anyone better in New York, the part's yours!'

Within weeks, I was headed home to Montreal and then on to New York to start rehearsing *Hadrian VII* on December 2, 1968. We opened on January 8, 1969, at the Helen Hayes Theatre on 46th Street, to glowing reviews. We were a hit. It was a wonderful cast; particularly Alec McCowen (as Hadrian), William Needles and Gillie Fenwick, both old friends from Toronto. After the show, we'd head west along 46th Street to Joe Allen's Restaurant or up 8th Avenue to the Haymarket. With eight shows a week, I settled into my life on Broadway. I rented myself a tiny apartment on West 12th Street in the West Village, where I already knew many people, and settled into going to movies during the day and whatever theatre performances I could see around my own weekly eight shows. Alec had already played

Hadrian for more than a year in London, and he had the right to leave the show after nine months. The producers hired Barry Morse, star of the TV series *The Fugitive* (and former AD of the Shaw Festival), who had played Hadrian in Australia, to replace Alec. But within a month it was obvious the show wouldn't survive, and *Hadrian* closed on November 15, 1969.

I headed back home to Montreal briefly and then on December 15, 1969, I flew to London, and on to the Birmingham Repertory Theatre. Artistic Director Peter Dews had offered me three plays; *Hamlet* where I'd play Horatio to Alec McCowen's Hamlet; *The Sorrows of Frederick* where I'd play Voltaire opposite John Wood as King Frederick the Great of Prussia; and Chekhov's *Three Sisters* where I'd play Tusenbach. It was great to be working with Alec again, and the company was very strong. I moved into the lower floor of a house with two Rep actors, (the British) Geoff Bowes and Richard Denning. Anna Massey and her boyfriend shared the upstairs flat. We'd all get together to have a roast most Sundays.

John Wood, a Broadway star, arrived and we started rehearsing *The Sorrows of Frederick*, a very interesting play by the American Southern author Romulus Linney (father of actor Laura Linney). This production was an early tryout for London and Broadway. New York producer Robert Whitehead arrived, with his wonderful wife, actress Zoe Caldwell, who'd played Cleopatra at Stratford in 1967. Ultimately, Robert wasn't able to put together a London or a New York production and *Frederick* closed on April 4, 1970. We opened *Three Sisters* on April 7. A very interesting production by Michael Simpson, it played through May 23, 1970. I then shared a house with Canadian actors Larry Aubrey and Richard Monette, on Crouch Hill, in northern London. The next week, I took a trip to St Tropez with two friends, Geraldine Sherman and Tommy Tune. We lounged on the beach, drank Rose de Provence and ate salade niçoise for the next ten days.

I'd been hired by the BBC to play defendant Rennie Davis in

their TV drama *The Chicago Conspiracy Trial*, and we had our first read-through on August 3, 1970. A group of New York actors had been imported for the production. James Patterson played lawyer William Kunstler, Robert Loggia played Davis's lawyer, Leonard Weinglass, Al Freeman Jr played Bobby Seale, Cliff Gorman played Abbie Hoffman and Morris Carnovsky played Judge Hoffman. After four weeks of rehearsal, we spent twelve hours taping the show in Studio T.C.4 at the Wood Lane TV Centre. At the same time that we were rehearsing the TV production, a stage production of the trial was being performed at Charles Marowitz's theatre in London, with William Burroughs playing Judge Hoffman.

My friend Dena Sherman was talking about leaving for New York, to join her friend Jimmy Hammerstein. As I watched the broadcast of *The Chicago Conspiracy Trial* (inclusive of an editorial from a real English judge telling the BBC audience that the British justice system could *never* produce anything like what had occurred in Judge Hoffman's courtroom), I decided to return to North America. Tommy Tune had just finished shooting Dean Martin's *Golddiggers in London* show, so we all flew over the Atlantic on December 7, 1970. After a week of partying with various New York friends, I flew up to Montreal to spend Christmas with my family. After the holiday, I returned to New York, to meet with my agent and talk about the future. To my surprise, he told me that the CBC wanted to fly me to Toronto to read for a television series they were preparing based on Mazo de la Roche's *Jalna* novels. I flew up to Toronto in January 1971, but I didn't feel I was right for the Jalna character I was asked to read. I had dinner with an old friend, theatre director Timothy Bond, who told me he was starting a film development company and he wanted me to write screenplays with him. It was such an intriguing idea, I ended up staying in Toronto, and started to write film scripts.

I started a second script on spec, about a murder on the Toronto subway (which was ultimately produced by Universal Pictures as *She*

Cried Murder, starring Telly Savalas) but what I needed was a well-paid acting job. I couldn't find anything until Tim Bond told me that theatre writer/director John Palmer was going to direct a new rock-musical about Charles Manson. The *New York Post* had been full of photos and stories about the Manson murders while I was doing *Hadrian VII* in 1969. And the latest *Rolling Stone* magazine was featuring Manson on its cover, with a long interview. Tim Bond invited John Palmer over for dinner and we talked about this musical, *Charles Manson: a.k.a Jesus Christ*. I had a previous connection with John. I'd been on a committee that had chosen a play of his, *Geobbels Gobbledygook*, as a production at the University Drama League Festival in 1965. I told him I'd love to read for the role of Manson. After we spent an afternoon together, John told me I had the part. The play would be produced at Theatre Passe Muraille in the fall of 1971.

I was about to enter a new world, at one of the most dynamic theatres in Canada.

SELECTED SOURCES

CHAPTER ONE

1. Interview with Jim Garrard, June 12, 1985, Metropolitan Toronto Library (MTL)
2. Rochdale Theatre Project, MTL microfiche
3. Garrard interview, June 12, 1985, MTL
4. Don Rubin, *Canadian Theatre Review 20*, Fall 1978
5. Garrard interview, June 12, 1985, MTL
6. Garrard quoted by Marci McDonald, *Toronto Star*, March 5, 1969

CHAPTER TWO

7. Garrard interview, June 12, 1985, MTL

CHAPTER THREE

8. Garrard interview, June 12, 1985, MTL
9. Theatre Passe Muraille history, MTL microfiche
10. Booth Savage interview, May 22, 1985
11. John Palmer interview, July 14, 1985
12. Don Rubin, *Toronto Star*, July 9, 1969

CHAPTER FOUR

13. Clare Coulter quoted in *Canadian Theatre Review 6*, Spring 1975
14. Henry Tarvainen quoted by Betty Lee, *Globe Magazine*, February 21, 1970
15. Paul Thompson interview, March 31, 1986

16. Thompson quoted by Herbert Whittaker, *Globe and Mail*, October 28, 1972
17. Thompson introduction to *Doukhobors* script, 1973
18. Thompson quoted by Paul Wilson, *Blyth Spirit*, April 1983
19. Thompson quoted by Linda West, *That's Show Business*, September 25, 1974
20. Thompson quoted by David Fox, interview, December 1, 1986
21. Thompson quoted by Herbert Whittaker, *Globe and Mail*, August 9, 1973
22. Thompson quoted by Frank Risky, *Toronto Star*, February 14, 1974
23. Thompson quoted by Debra Sharp, *Globe and Mail*, October 13, 1979
24. Thompson quoted by Frank Risky, *Toronto Star*, November 5, 1974
25. Thompson quoted by Linda West, *That's Show Business*, September 25, 1974
26. Thompson quoted by Ted Johns, *Canadian Theatre Review* 13, Winter 1977 (other quotes follow)
27. Quoted by Candace Bullard, *New York Theatre Journal* 5, #2, Winter 1976
28. Linda Griffiths, introduction to *Maggie and Pierre*, Talon Books, 1980

Photo credit: Marion Lewis

PETER JOBIN was an actor and writer who participated in Canadian theatre and film for over fifty years. Born in Montreal, he appeared in plays in Canada, the USA and the UK before beginning a career as a screenwriter. He is known for films such as *Happy Birthday to Me* (1981) and *Diamond Cut Diamond* (2001). Peter died August 8, 2018.

Photo credit: Robert Nasmith

LIONEL DOUGLAS was a major force during the glory days of Rochdale. A master raconteur and polymath, he could work a room like nobody's business, and had an amazing vision of all that was not yet done. He loved photography and Ducati motorcycles. The former you will enjoy in these pages, the latter killed him.

Photo credit: Lionel Douglas

ROBERT NASMITH was, briefly, president of Rochdale and a photographer. Most of his photographic work (both his work as a combat photographer in Vietnam and his later work) did not survive the whips and scorns of time, but his association with Theatre Passe Muraille as an artist and board member has lasted forty-eight years. He is quite a good actor.

Photo credit: Cylla Von Tiedemann

DAVID FERRY is a dramaturge and sometime designer and an award-winning actor and director living in Toronto.

He has been published as a writer himself and has edited a collection of plays by James Reaney with a bibliography: *Reaney Days in the West Room: Seven Plays by James Reaney* for Playwrights Canada Press (Toronto, 2009). He also edited *He Speaks: Monologues for Men* for Playwrights Canada Press (Toronto, 2008) and co-edited *Making a Scene* for Playwrights Canada Press (Toronto, 1985–2010). His audio collection *Canajun, eh?* of Canadian dialects as a resource for actors is still available on CD.

I Love You, Baby Blue. Set, 1975.

Photo courtesy of R. Nasmith Archives.